LOVE ON THE ROCKS

Stories of Rusticators and Romance on Mount Desert Island

by John and Kathryn Muether

Also from Islandport Press

Live Free and Eat Pie: A Storyteller's Guide to New Hampshire
by Rebecca Rule

Billy Boy by Jean Mary Flahive

My Life in the Maine Woods by Annette Jackson

Contentment Cove by Miriam Colwell

Young by Miriam Colwell

Stealing History by William D. Andrews

Shoutin' into the Fog by Thomas Hanna

down the road a piece: A Storyteller's Guide to Maine
by John McDonald

A Moose and a Lobster Walk into a Bar by John McDonald

Windswept by Mary Ellen Chase

Mary Peters by Mary Ellen Chase

Silas Crockett by Mary Ellen Chase

Nine Mile Bridge by Helen Hamlin

In Maine by John N. Cole

The Cows Are Out! by Trudy Chambers Price

Hauling by Hand by Dean Lawrence Lunt

At One: In a Place Called Maine
by Lynn Plourde and Leslie Mansmann

The Little Fisherman by Margaret Wise Brown and Dahlov Ipcar

Titus Tidewater by Suzy Verrier

*A is for Acadi*a by Richard Johnson and Ruth Gortner Grierson

These and other Maine books are available at:
www.islandportpress.com

To J + B

LOVE ON THE ROCKS

Stories of Rusticators and Romance on Mount Desert Island

by John and Kathryn Muether

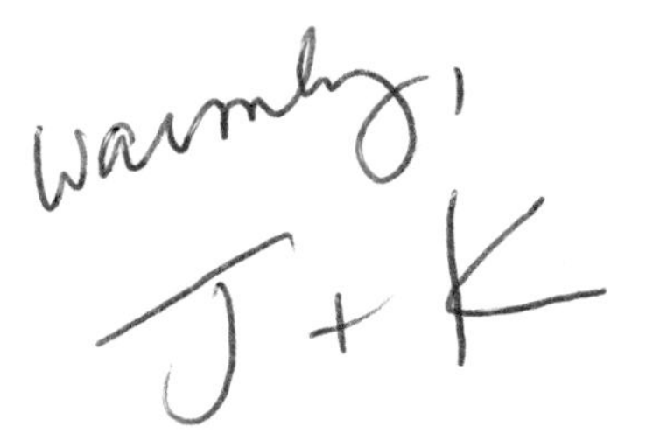

Islandport Press • Frenchboro • Yarmouth

Islandport Press
P.O. Box 10
Yarmouth, Maine 04096

www.islandportpress.com

ISBN: 978-1-934031-18-6
Library of Congress Control Number: 2008929757

First edition published July 2008

Book design by Michelle Lunt / Islandport Press
Cover Design by Karen Hoots / Mad Hooter Design

Front and back cover photographs from the collection of Raymond Strout.

Dedication

Elizabeth Hill Cram (1905–1995) was a longtime summer resident of Mount Desert Island who started us on the literary adventure that produced this book. Her charming tales of island life became our entrée into this world, and her rich personal library deepened our affection for the region and its heritage. This book is dedicated to her memory.

Introduction

Mount Desert, the home of Acadia National Park, is an island, as a study of a map will make plain. But it is much more than that, and the water that surrounds it is not the only key to its charm and popularity. It is also circumscribed by mystery, legend, and romance. For centuries, this island paradise has attracted explorers, seafarers, farmers, artists, and tourists.

And also its share of writers. In his introduction to Sargent Collier's book, *Green Grows Bar Harbor*, Cleveland Amory observed that over the years Mount Desert Island and its principal town not only established an artistic reputation, but a literary tradition as well. "In its early days," wrote Amory, "the novelists marked it for their own—the 'Bar Harbor novel' became almost the same kind of staple reading fare in the upper echelons that the 'dime novel' became farther down the literary ladder." Amory elaborated on this claim in his own study of Bar Harbor social life, found in his book, *The Last Resorts*:

> *All the great social resorts have been thoroughly exploited as backgrounds for novels, but no resort ever captured the fancy of as many novelists as Bar Harbor. In the early-day novels, there is endless "calling" as well as an almost incessant "tinkle of the tea things." The cottage library is the general trysting place, but the characters also move slowly back and forth, among page-length paragraphs of scenery, between fields and streams, drawing rooms and verandas.*

As Amory noted, Mount Desert Island has long captured the American literary imagination, and it may be fairly said that writers, just as much as artists, have "invented Acadia." It has been as fertile a place for the pen as it has for the brush, even to the point of establishing a unique literary genre in the "Bar Harbor novel."

Typically, the Bar Harbor novel records the great cottage days of that town, as the nineteenth century draws to a close. It begins on a steamship headed for Mount Desert in June, and it ends happily ever after (or in September, whichever comes first). In between there are elaborate descriptions of the breathtaking natural surroundings but little in terms of a plot. Despite Charles Warner's claim that Bar Harbor is "the finest sanitorium for flirtations," we find, in Marion Crawford's apt words, a lot of "love in idleness." The idleness often occurs on the island's granite coast, to the point of the coinage of the local term "rocking" to refer to the slow summer courtships. Other characteristic scenes involve buckboards and especially canoes, as Sargent Collier and Tom Horgan explain: "from a chaperonage point of view, canoeing was considered a safe activity, since an oversized swain could easily be controlled in such an unstable craft."

Love on the Rocks aims to present the mystery and romance of the island's bygone era for modern readers. It includes eleven samples, written over the span of three decades in the latter half of the nineteenth century. Some of the writers were professional authors; others were amateurs whose experience of Bar Harbor prompted literary ambitions. As Constance Harrison expressed it, "to begin writing about Bar Harbor and the joys it has brought to our life, of the interesting and memorable entertainments we gave and received there, and the delightful people who yearly drifted to the island, is to want not to lay by one's pen."

Not all of these selections follow the formula of the Bar Harbor novel. Many are not even novels; the anthology includes short stories, a poem, and a play. But each of these samples, the reader will discover, is steeped in the intoxication of the Gilded Age pilgrims as they discovered the beauty of the island and the gaiety of its social scene. The arrangement of the material is chronological, thus giving a sense of the evolution of the island as a tourist Mecca, from the post–Civil War invasion of steamships to the height of its extravagant hotel and cottage life.

In the twentieth century, automobiles, income tax, and ultimately, the Bar Harbor fire of 1947 would bring that way of life to an end, along with the literature that described it. Over a century later, however, the island has not lost its power to charm. With the establishment of Acadia National Park, Mount Desert Island continues to attract millions of visitors every summer, and most of them leave wishing that their brief stay could be extended. This anthology makes it possible to live year-round on Mount Desert Island, at least in one's literary imagination.

To begin writing about Bar Harbor and the joys it has brought into our life, of the interesting and memorable entertainments we gave and received there, and the delightful people who yearly drifted to the island, is to want not to lay by one's pen.

—Constance C. Harrison *(1843–1920)*

Table of Contents

Chapter 1

Caleb's Lark

Jane G. Austin

1868

A Boston workaholic is persuaded to take a much-needed vacation on "a little island off the coast of Maine," with all the necessary amenities, including fresh mackerel, blueberries, and the "prettiest women in the Union."

"Caleb's Lark" was originally published in The Atlantic Monthly *22 (December 1868): 652–63.*

"But, doctor, what shall we do for him? He laughs at medicine, dieting, and rest, and, like the late lamented Confederacy, only desires to be let alone—a treatment likely to be as fatal in this case as in that. What can I do for him?"

"Try a lark," sententiously replied the family physician, with a twinkle of his honest eyes.

"A lark!" dubiously echoed Miselle. "But where is one to be found? How would a robin answer?"

"Pho, child! not a lark to eat, but a lark to do, to be, and to suffer. Recreation," said the doctor; and Miselle put on her considering-cap.

"I have it!" exclaimed she, presently. "Not a cent for himself, millions for someone else—that's Caleb! Doctor, tell him confidentially that my health is suffering for want of rest and change. Advise him to take me somewhere directly; and leave the rest of the case to me."

The doctor nodded, smiled, and took his leave.

That evening Caleb casually remarked to the wife of his bosom: "Miselle, I have been thinking that I should enjoy a little trip to the mountains or the seashore. What do you say to the idea?"

"Anything that pleases you, my dear," meekly replied Miselle. "When would you like to go? I have just been reading a glowing account of Mount Desert, a little island off the coast of Maine, which seems to combine everything desirable in a holiday-ground—lofty mountains, deep ravines, forests, precipices, gorges, echoes, fresh mackerel, and no end of blueberries; in fact, all the delicacies of the season, including the prettiest women in the Union, who are there collected."

"What magnificent combinations!" exclaimed Caleb, in enthusiasm. "Mackerel and sunset skies, blueberries and ocean, alike unlimited, pretty women and nature! The antitheses are irresistible. Miselle, go pack your trunk." Which command was obeyed with such zeal, that at 6 P.M. upon the succeeding evening the pleasure-seekers left Boston by rail for Portland, there to take boat for Mount Desert; preferring this mode of transit to making the entire passage by water, as some persons choose to do. Reaching Portland at 10 P.M., travelers and luggage were quietly transferred to the steamer *Lewiston*, a pretty and commodious boat under admirable management.

"Sit here while I look for our stateroom," directed Caleb, leaving Miselle *planté* before a divan divided by arms into sections like a pie. Most of these sections were occupied by persons wearing the preternaturally solemn expression of incipient seasickness, and Miselle, leaving her satchel and sunshade to keep them company, made her independent way to the forward deck, when a sudden tornado snatched and bore away her hat, whisked her drapery into undignified and ungraceful festoons, and made of her own hair a veil to cover her confusion, as she hastily retreated from the group of smokers among whom she had plunged, and penitently sought countenance and protection among her discreeter sisters upon the divan, now in the rigid condition preceding the final agony of *maladie-du-mer*.

Here Caleb presently found, wondered at, mildly rebuked, and finally bore away, the hatless and disheveled aspirant for fresh air, for once quite subdued and silent.

After leaving Rockland—a thriving town at the mouth of the Penobscot River, where the passengers coming from Boston by boat are received on board the *Lewiston*—the route lies among the myriad islands of the coast of Maine, and every curve of the sinuous course opens a new vista of combined land and ocean view positively startling in its wild beauty. Many of these islands, as well as various points upon the mainland, perpetuate in their names the memory of French discovery and occupation—as Castine, where an old French fort still towers above an earthwork not yet five years old; the islands of Grand and Petit Manan, Terre Haute, Belle Isle, Isle au Haut, Rosier, and Mount Desert, itself originally *Mont Desart*, although some antiquarians choose to derive the name from that of Captain Dessertes, one of the first navigators of Frenchman's Bay.

But resolutely closing ears and eyes to the bewildering and bewitching traditions so artfully mingled with the history of this island that one knows not whether to visit first Gold-Diggers Glen, where several enthusiastic speculators are today searching for Captain Kyd's buried treasure, or to search at Fernald's Point for the still more apocryphal site of the old Jesuit settlement established under the patronage of the fair and discreet Madame de Guercheville about 1613, and so cruelly destroyed by an English governor of Virginia named Argall some years later, Miselle returns to her simple narrative of personal experience, leaving the glory of research and compilation to more industrious historians.

"Come and see Mount Desert. We are just going into Southwest Harbor," said Caleb, and Miselle, closing her book, followed to the bows of the steamer to look upon a view wonderful in its savage beauty; for the great mountains standing sentry at either side the port were clothed in dense evergreen forest, and the valleys between them seemed wells of darkness. Black thunderclouds, gathering upon the crests of the hills, spread rapidly over the sky, until now so smiling; so that at last the whole island lay in frowning shadow, while the sea far to southward still glittered in summer sunshine, and the *Lewiston*, with her freight, seemed a veritable Charon's boat bringing hapless souls from the warmth and light of life to some dim, horribly beautiful purgatory, beyond which might lie heaven or hell.

"Only, six dollars is a good deal more than an obolus," remarked Miselle, the nineteenth century pressing hard upon her.

"What is that? Why, it is raining, as sure as I'm a sinner!" responded Caleb.

"Don't speak of it now, if you are," murmured Miselle, following him across the gangway plank to a wharf surrounded by lobster-canning factories, and redolent of fish. Here stood sundry remarkable vehicles, into one of which Miselle found herself hastily packed, in company with a jolly cripple, two limp and despairing women, and a driver; while Caleb, who had four times secured a seat and relinquished it to whoever would accept it, plodded cheerfully along in the rain, and stood waiting, like an aqueous angel, to receive his charge upon the steps of Deacon Clark's Hotel. Beside him was the Deacon himself, grave, benevolent, and patriarchal, while behind them appeared the cheery faces of the Friend from Philadelphia, and the Count all the way from Germany; for—again like Hades—Mount Desert collects its visitors from all the world.

"Very glad to see you. Dinner is ready," said the Deacon with a nice adaptation of the topic to the mood of his guests; and the rest of the day was devoted to a blazing fire, conversation, both merry and grave, teatime, and plans for the morrow. But Miselle closed her weary eyes to the lullaby of the rain upon the roof, and awoke to the same melody. A breakfast, graced by the freshest of mackerel and the sweetest of blueberries, mitigated, but could not conceal, the fact that the rainy morning was likely to continue into a rainy day. From the table the party adjourned to the piazza.

"What a pity that we must lose the walk to Big Pond this morning!" said the Friend, mildly appealing to the uncompromising clouds.

"I'm going," announced Miselle; "I shall be ready in fifteen minutes."

"But it rains," remonstrated the Count.

"So I see."

"You will get awfully wet," suggested Caleb.

Far up the height of the steep stairs, Miselle's voice replied, "In fifteen minutes."

But fortune favors the brave, and when, in less than the prescribed quarter of an hour, the party set forth, equipped with rubber boots and overcoats, waterproof cloaks and umbrellas, while Caleb paid unusual deference to the elements by fastening one button of his coat, the clouds had broken and the rain had ceased. Three miles of bush and brake, woodland road, and wood without road, brought the explorers to Big Pond, or Long Lake, the indigenous and imported names of a lovely sheet of water shut in by Beech Hill Mountain on the right and Western on the left, while the southern end is finished by the little sandy beach to be found, as the Friend asserts, at the southern end of every lake upon the island.

Upon this beach sat down the four, breathless, draggled, and happy. Beside them crisped and murmured a little woodland brook, tumbling across the sands toward the lake; above them floated the clouds, now breaking to show a watery sun, now gathering stern and dark upon the mountain summits. The evergreen forests clothing the hillsides were full of mystery and gloom; but creeping out from their shadow, and holding the middle ground between forest and beach, rioted the wild convolvulus, the brilliant scarlet bunchberry, the sweet blue harebells, and clusters of the loveliest wild roses that ever bloomed on earth. Upon the beach lay scattered the bleached trunks of trees far larger than the present growth of the hills; and the Count argued, with much show of reason, that they were the metamorphosed remains of Titanic heroes who had fought and died upon these shores, upheaving hills and hollowing lake basins in the ardor of their mighty struggle.

"I should say, rather," gravely suggested Caleb, "that these smaller trunks are the remains of the heroes, while the larger ones represent the hippogriffs, sylants, or other battle-chargers which they bestrode. This upon which we sit would, for instance, have served as steed for Hengist himself."

"Yes, it is without doubt the *Streit hengst* of that renowned warrior," replied the Count, examining the relic from which the party reverently arose.

"The theory is a good one, but does not the *Streit hengst* of Hengist sound rather tautological?" mildly inquired the Friend.

"Never mind tautology; let us roll the *Streit hengst* into the lake! Let us hasten his resolution into the elements! Let us offer him a sacrifice to Odin and to Thor! Above all, let us amuse ourselves!" shouted the Count, throwing off his coat, and picking up a small stick.

The ribs of heroes make excellent levers, their mighty vertebrae serve capitally as fulcrums; and in a few moments the whole party, Miselle included, were laboring at their task with might and main, regardless of the clouds mustering yet more darkly upon Beech Hill, and even of the raindrops dimpling the bosom of the lake like the bullets of sharp-shooters.

"There!" cried Caleb, giving the *Streit hengst* a final impetus, and flinging after him the rib of Hengist which had affected it. "We have fulfilled our duty to the past, now let us think of the present. Miselle, child, assert your femininity, and be afraid of the rain directly."

Such a merry race homeward! Such scrambling toilets! Such Homeric appetites for so nice a dinner, not yet ended when Deacon Clark announced that a return carriage was about to start for Bar Harbor, and would be glad of passengers! The opportunity was a good one, so, after brief consultation, the travelers abandoned for the time the remaining lions of Southwest Harbor, bundled their wet clothes into the trunks with their dry ones, paid the Deacon's bill, silently wondering to what use so guileless a patriarch could put so much money, and set forth upon their drive.

The road from Southwest Harbor to Bar Harbor is set down as sixteen miles in length. To this may be added some five or six miles of perpendicular ascent and precipitous descent; the latter remarkably exhilarating for strong nerves, but rather trying to weak ones, especially as the horses are encouraged to make the descents at full speed, and the pitch of the carriage and clatter of roiling stones become something really awful.

Upon the brink of one of these precipices the driver checked his horses, and looked back into the carriage with an expectant grin.

"Oh!" remarked the Friend, "hallo-o-o-o-o-o!"

"Has he gone mad?" whispered Miselle, clinging to Caleb; but the Count held up his finger, imploring silence, while back from the broad breast of Beech Hill Mountain, and over the placid lake at its foot, came the response, clear, sweet, and powerful.

Having thus summoned the nymph, the Friend gracefully introduced his friends, and withdrew, leaving them to continue the conversation, which they did with great satisfaction; Echo sweetly replying to every appeal, whether it were an operatic refrain in Caleb's mellow tones, a thunderous German apostrophe from the Count, a bit of sisterly *badinage* in Miselle's treble, or bovine bellow of the driver.

About halfway from Southwest to Bar Harbor lies the village of Somesville, or, as the post office will have it, the town of Mount Desert, and Miselle here pauses to give the traveling public a hint in the matter of mail addresses upon this island. A letter intended for Southwest Harbor should be superscribed Tremont, Maine; one for Somesville, Mount Desert, Maine; and one for Bar Harbor, East Eden, Maine—these being the names of the three towns, while the others are mere local sobriquets, to be added or omitted at pleasure. The name of Mount Desert, however, should never be added unless it is desired that the letters should arrive at Somesville. But with all or any of these precautions the subject of postal communication is enveloped in the same romantic cloud shrouding the rest of Mount Desert matters, and refuses to be reduced to arbitrary rules or certainties.

The principal feature of Somesville is Somes Sound, an arm of the sea some seven miles in length by one in width, nearly cutting the island in halves, and so straight that from its head one may look down its shining path to the sea horizon leagues beyond. Besides the sound, Somesville boasts mountain scenery so fine that the little inn is always filled with artists, their portfolios crammed with "studies" for next winter's pictures, and their faces beaming with wonder and delight. More than all, Somesville boasts the aristocrat of the island in the person of Captain Somes, who with his pretty daughters keeps the village inn, and reigns patriarchally today over the acres his fathers possessed and named two centuries before the Shoddies, the Gunnybags, and the McFlimsies ever heard of Mount Desert. Also, may Somesville boast a variety store, where hats can be procured for such unfortunates as have lost their own, a town pump, and a very promising and observant crop of future presidents and presidentesses.

Leaving Somesville, the travelers were presently called upon to admire the prospect from the Saddle, a name bestowed upon the highest point of land crossed by the road, and from whence may be obtained a fine view of nearly the entire island, embracing Marsh, Western, Beech Hill, Dog, Sargent's, Wasgott, and Sharp mountains at the western extremity, and Green, Dry, Bubble, and Newport at the eastern, not to mention various lovely water glimpses of ocean, sound, lake, and brooklet, and some of the finest forest scenery imaginable; for in the woods of Maine grow and thrive in lusty beauty the arborvitae, the fir balsam, the hemlock, the hop-hornbeam, moosewood, and many another sylvan treasures only found with us of the more southern latitudes in nurseries or upon carefully tended lawns.

After the Saddle came a hurried visit to Eagle Lake, a beautiful sheet of water lying at the foot of Green Mountain, and reflecting the great hill in its placid waters.

"The little sandy beach at the southern end still, you remark," said the Friend, as the party returned to their carriage.

Another half hour, and the travelers, cold, weary, wet, and hungry, arrived in Bar Harbor, and stiffly dismounted at the door of Captain Hamor's hospitable house, whereat stood the gallant Captain himself, who, after brief survey, led his guests to the only fire in the house, albeit it blazed in the kitchen stove, and, seating them thereby, commanded, "Some warm supper for these folks right away."

An epicurean writer advises: "If you would eat beefsteak, sit beside the fire with a warm plate, and let the cook toss the meat from the gridiron into it."

To which Miselle appends: "If you would eat fish, travel all day in a northeasterly storm, and sit beside the stove to see it fried, listening, meanwhile, to the story of its capture within the hour."

Supper over—for no such aesthetic title as tea describes the banquet of fish, meat, corn bread, white biscuit, toast, blueberries, cake, doughnuts, and cheese, spread before Caleb and his friends—the Captain announced, with some hesitation, that the accommodations of his house being limited, a large number of his guests were obliged to lodge out; and that for this particular party had been secured rooms in a certain cottage just along shore, where it was hoped they might be comfortable.

"A cottage by the sea," murmured Miselle, quite ready to be charmed with the proposed abode, and not the less so for finding it was to be shared by some old friends, the General and his wife, just from Washington.

"The first thing to do is to visit Schooner Head and Great Head," announced the Friend next morning at breakfast; and the party, electing him *cicerone*, were presently packed in a big wagon in company with Chibiabos the sweet singer, and Atalanta his wife, who for once condescended to employ horse's feet instead of her own active members.

Caleb assumed the reins, and the roan was already in motion when a hail from the artist arrested them.

"Beg pardon, but they say you are going to Schooner Head."

"Yes."

"Then let me tell you the road is absolutely impassable. There is one gully a hundred feet long, three or four deep; and extending from one side of the road to the other. There is no getting through, by, or over it."

The party looked at each other.

"I suppose, then, we must give it up," said the men.

"What fun! Let us go on!" exclaimed the women; to which Miselle added in an aside, "This is where the 'lark' comes in, Caleb."

The stronger minds prevailed, as they should; and, with thanks to the artist, the party drove merrily out of the gate and along a road as full of picturesque beauty as of holes, and presenting as startling a variety of scenery as of impediment. Like some of the young gentlemen who finish their education abroad, the farther it went the worse it grew, until all minor atrocities ended at the mouth of the gully, which in appearance quite justified the character bestowed upon it by the artist.

A council of war was held, resulting in the roan's being slipped from the shafts, and prevailed upon to scramble down and through the gully to its farther termination, where he was entrusted to Atalanta and Miselle, with strictest orders to all three to remain precisely where they were left, and attempt no ambitious operations whatever—orders minutely obeyed by both roan and his keepers until the controlling element was out of sight, when they at once followed to a point commanding the field of action, which they contemplated with gleeful satisfaction.

"Just fancy those men laboring in that style from necessity instead of for fun," suggested Atalanta, as she watched Chibiabos, the Friend, the Count, and Caleb, who, literally putting their shoulders to the wheel, pushed, pulled, lifted, and hoisted the heavy wagon along, conclusively proving that four men are *almost* equal to one horse.

The gully, however, was passed; the picket-guard, duly chidden for disobedience and insubordinate mirth, was relieved of its charge; the roan reharnessed; the party repacked; and the journey continued over a road still very bad, but leading through a region of such wild beauty that its faults were all forgiven. The last part of its course lay under the eastern side of Newport Mountain, which, like nearly every other mountain upon the island, slopes gradually and greenly to the west, and toward the east presents a precipitous and frowning face of naked granite. Another curious feature in this formation is the fact that several of these precipitous mountain faces terminate in water—either lake, sound, or ocean. Of a sudden the broken road disappeared altogether, and we came upon a grassy plateau, with a fisherman's cottage at its farther extremity and a landlocked harbor beyond, beautiful enough to have sheltered Cleopatra's galleys, instead of the unsavory fishing craft riding at anchor there.

"Do you see that sheer precipice near the crest of Newport?" asked the Friend, helping Miselle from the wagon.

"Yes. Has it a story?"

"Some years ago two girls were scrambling along its edge—looking for berries, I believe—when one fell over, dragging her comrade after her. The first crashed straight down upon the rocks, two hundred feet below, and never stirred again. The other fell upon her, and escaped with broken limbs and terrible bruises. Her shrieks were heard at this house, and some men went immediately to the rescue; but such was the difficulty, at first of reaching, and afterward of removing her, that it was eight hours before she was raised to the edge of the cliff. Fancy those eight hours!"

"But did she live?"

"Oh yes, and is today landlady of one of the Bar Harbor hotels. Humanity is so absurdly tenacious of life. But the roan is safely stabled in the fence-corner, and Atalanta leads the way to Schooner Head."

So through the great gate, and over the oozy meadow path, gay with harebells and wild roses, up a sharp ascent, and along a slippery crag-path, trooped the merry party, until, reaching the brow of a mighty cliff, they found the ocean at their feet, filling the far horizon with his splendor. Beside them lay the Spouting Horn—a mighty cauldron, a hundred feet or more in depth, into which the sea has worn an entrance through a layer of softer rock near the base of the dividing cliff, and where, having gained admittance, it fights and rages, like any trapped wild thing, to regain its liberty. To the roar of the rising wave succeeds the moan and swirl of the retreating one, and then the wild struggle between the incoming and outgoing forces, until one closing his eyes might fancy himself lying beside the veritable mouth of the pit, as described by Bunyan.

"Rameses, as you call him," said the Friend, "clambered down the inside of the Horn at low tide, until he could look through the arch out to the open sea."

"I should like to have heard his next sermon," commented Miselle, graciously allowing Caleb to make of his knee a step in the somewhat perilous descent from the Horn to the cliff whence one may see the outer entrance of the cave. Here, seated upon a convenient shelf, with the waters now swelling to their feet, now lapsing until the dripping cliffs lay bare and black beneath, the friends spent a happy hour before they thought of time. Just over the surface of the gulf, where the waves flew back from the face of the cliff in showers of spray, appeared and vanished at every moment the ghost of a rainbow. High overhead rose the cliffs, whose resemblance, as viewed from seaward, to a schooner with all sail set, has given the place its name. High in the blue zenith sailed an eagle, his broad vans motionless, while far below him whirled and screamed a flock of snow-white gulls. The bright waters of the bay were studded with sails, and the stately ships went on to some fair unknown haven, when—

"Suppose we get a lunch at Norriss's, and take the whole afternoon for Great Head?" suggested the poet of the party.

The proposition was hailed as a brilliant one, and, the spell being broken, everyone found himself ready to return to the little house at the head of the bay, where the lunch was ordered; and during its preparation a part of the company found time to visit a curious cave upon the shore, known as the Devil's Oven, and celebrated for the number and variety of its sea anemones and other marine treasures; while their more indolent or weary companions chose rather to sit beside the open fire, watch the manufacture and baking of cakes and pies in a "tin reflector," and listen to anecdotes and reminiscences from the elders of the family who have lived, married, come into and gone out of the world in this secluded spot for many a year before the world came to surprise them with the news that it was famous.

The cakes baked, and the wanderers returned, the lunch, or rather dinner, since salted fish formed one of its elements, was served, and eaten with a relish not always conceded to Blot's or Soyer's most successful efforts. The roan, having also dined, was favored with a draught of water from Atalanta's botanical specimen box; and the party, resuming their places, drove merrily on through a pretty wood road, in the direction of Great Head. Another isolated house, seated at the head of a lovely little golden beach, marks the end of the carriage roan; and while the gentlemen once more unharnessed and stabled the roan, Atalanta and Miselle entered, and made acquaintance with the hospitable dame, while Capitoliana, Britomarte, Hatty Louise, Wilfred, and Conins tumbled about the floor, or peered in at the guests with wide eyes of wonder glowing beneath a thatch of sunburned hair.

"Your children have quite romantic names; where did you find them?" inquired Miselle, mildly resisting Hatty Louise's efforts to wrench open her watch-case.

"Out of the *New York Ledger*, ma'am," replied the complacent mother. "Me and my sister and another lady club together and take it; and I think it's most a beautiful paper—don't you, ma'am?"

"Much better than nothing," sensibly replied Atalanta, while Miselle hesitated; and then, as Caleb's head appeared at the open window, they took leave, and followed the Friend, who acted as guide, through about a mile of flowery woodland path, coming at last upon the black crags of Great Head, the answering promontory to Schooner Head, and yet more massive and imposing in its structure. The party scattered over the surface of the cliff, and Miselle, finding a little nook close at the water's edge, sat watching in silent delight the grand march of the waves, as sweeping up, battalion after battalion, they fearlessly dashed themselves to foam against the gray old rocks which for ages have borne the assault as unflinchingly as now, and shall endure in primeval strength and majesty when we who marvel have passed on to meet yet greater marvels.

One noticeable point in this view is its primitive character. Seated low in the amphitheater of the cliff nothing is visible but sea, sky, and rock; not one flower, one blade of grass, or even the brown earth, is to be seen. It is a glimpse of the era before the lichens had turned to moss, or the *parvenu* man had yet been dreamed of. Near the crest of the cliff is a profile rock nearly as good as the famous Franconian one; but, when one goes so far to escape the constant sight of real profiles, why waste time or enthusiasm upon an imperfect imitation?

"Half past five, and a bad seven miles between us and the tea table," announced Caleb; and with many a backward look the friends departed, leaving the gray old cliff smiling rosily in the light of a glorious sunset, while all the east was filled with the silver and azure of moonrise.

With the morning came the sisters, fresh, sparkling, and energetic as morning itself.

"Gouldsboro! It is the very day for it—a favorable tide, a promising wind, and Captain Royal Higgins disengaged," said Roma, while Avoca quietly put Miselle's bow straight, adding, "and we will dine at Captain Hill's, and drive to Sullivan."

"Oh, sailing! How can anyone speak of sailing at Mount Desert after that dreadful, dreadful accident last summer! Did you hear of it?" cried Dame Partlett with an anxious glance toward her own ducklings.

"But we are going with Captain Higgins," said Roma, in a sufficing sort of way; and while the dame proceeded with the melancholy tale of the wreck and loss of every life but one out of a party of eleven, Roma supplemented the story of Captain Higgins's prompt and courageous action in the matter, resulting in the saving of that one life, and establishing an enviable reputation as man and sailor for himself.

So the voyage to Gouldsboro was arranged, and a party made up, including the four friends, the General, his wife, and Dick, the sisters, the ambassador, the two English ladies, the *fiancée* and Mephistopheles. A party selected as it should be, with every one capable of contributing something to the general enjoyment; for "even I can serve as ballast," remarked Caleb, seating himself with much satisfaction between Roma and Avoca, while Miselle, with Captain Higgins's quiet connivance, established herself in the little skiff towing behind the *Petrel* and enjoyed the atom of danger and full draught of exhilaration incident to her position hugely.

Gouldsboro upon the map means a town some twelve miles east of Mount Desert, occupying a peninsula between Frenchman's and Gouldsboro Bays. But Gouldsboro in the annals of Caleb's Lark means a quaint old-fashioned farmhouse, buried in riotous woodbine, and framed in a border of lilac and syringa bushes, sweet peas and marigolds, hollyhocks, sunflowers, poppies, southern wood, Ragged Robin, Love-lies-bleeding, and Johnny-jump-up-and-kiss-me, while from house and garden slopes to the water's edge a green and blossomy lawn. Seated in the porch of this old house, and feeding your senses with the perfume of the flowers, the songs of birds, and hum of bees, and wash of waves upon the shore, you may satisfy your soul with such a glorious view as hundreds of miles of travel cannot rival. Description could but do it injustice; and Miselle leaves to some future Murray the catalogue of islands studding the blue bay, some dark with evergreens, some bright with birch and alder growths, the mountain peaks crowding the horizon, the sails of every variety of craft, the soft pastoral beauty of the foreground. Or, pending the Murray, she introduces with pleasure to an appreciative public the genius of the spot, Captain Barney Hill, who "man and boy, has lived here and hereabouts this sixty year," and knows its story thoroughly.

From this feast Miselle was summoned to the less satisfying, but yet essential, banquet of fish and lamb, inevitable at the seashore, and here met with a delightful surprise in the person of her charming kinswoman, whose talk of the last book, the last music, the last idea of the thinkers, and last whim of the fashionists, added the same fanciful charm to the scene that her dainty gloves and handkerchief and fan did to the moss-grown and rough-hewn step upon which they lay.

The drive to Sullivan, along the shores of the bay, and giving a fine view of Mount Desert and the other islands upon the one hand and the inland country with the Schoodic Mountains upon the other, is described as something wonderful; but Captain Hill's horses having already gone in another direction, the party were obliged to content themselves with a pretty walk, a row upon the pond, and a harvest of water lilies. Then came good-bye to Gouldsboro and the fair cousin, who remained like Ariadne alone upon the shore, while the *Petrel*, sailing out into the sunset, carried its happy crew upon a voyage as full of romance and beauty as theirs who in the unremembered years sought for the Fortunate Isles.

Deep in the moonlit night the *Petrel* dropped anchor at her usual berth; and her passengers, full of content and peace, went each to his own abode.

The next day was devoted to the ascent of Green Mountain, the highest peak upon the island, measuring very nearly two thousand feet by actual survey, and the one spot of all others which a tourist may not omit visiting. After this, he may, if strong of limb and energy, scramble up Newport, and get a view much extolled by those who have seen it; or, like Atalanta, cross half a dozen mountains and valleys to Jordan's Pond, a spot whose beauty and inaccessibility are matters not to be put in words.

For pedestrians of moderate powers, however, the road up Green Mountain offers sufficient exertion to satisfy either conscience or spinal system. It can be accomplished by horsepower, if one is neither timid nor sympathetic with the brute creation; but the wisest course is to drive along the southwest harbor road about two miles to the beginning of the mountain road, where stands a guide-board to inform the public with suspicious exactness that the Summit House is distant two miles and an eighth—the eighth being a trope, or poetical figure, expressive of unknown and illimitable distance, capable of mitigation, however, by frequent rests upon mossy logs or shaded rocks, draughts from a clear cold spring, handsful of bunchberries and bluebells, and mouthsful of blueberries and mountain cranberries.

The Summit House, reached at length, proved to be a very comfortable cottage of primitive construction, but furnishing tolerable beds and a very good dinner.

"And *now*, Caleb, you may show me the view," graciously announced Miselle; and Caleb, who had employed the hour devoted by that young woman to repose in getting himself up as *cicerone*, proceeded, spyglass in hand, to do the honors of Green Mountain.

"In the first place you notice that we seem to be in the hollow of a great basin, with the sea rising in a blue slope upon every side until the horizon line is on a level with our eyes. This is on account of our great elevation above the sea level and is an effect often mentioned by aeronauts."

"Caleb! Did I come to the top of Green Mountain to imbibe Learning-made-easy? You will be attempting next to teach me the multiplication table."

"Excuse me, my dear, I never should attempt that; and I will now confine myself to obvious facts, leaving their attendant theories to you. Do you see that black beetle with a plume upon his head, crawling up the blue slope toward the horizon?"

"Yes, I see the beetle."

"Well, his, or rather her, name is *Lewiston*; and she is a steamer of no matter how many tons, proceeding from Southwest Harbor toward Machias. Through the spyglass you can distinguish the people upon her decks."

"Then I won't look through the glass, for I much prefer the black-beetle idea to the steamer idea. But where are all the ships gone today?"

"There are two ships and a good many other vessels in sight," replied Caleb with mild accuracy, "although I daresay you took them for boats, or even sea fowl; all those flashing white specks are sails. Now look at the islands. This, with a great bay eating the heart out of it, and leaving only a circle of earth, is called—"

"The Doge's Ring—is it not?"

"No more than Frenchman's Bay is called Adriatic. That is Great Cranberry—pronounced Crarmb'ry Island—and the nearer ones are Little Cranberries. Beyond is Long Island, and just above, if your eyes are very sharp, you can make out a speck called Mount Desert Rock. Stay, look through the glass at it. There is no danger of seeing any of your fellow creatures, although two of them inhabit it."

"A lighthouse? Oh yes; I make out a solitary shaft with a pedestal of rock and the foam dashing over it. Do you say two men live there? Why, it is worse than Minot Light."

"More lonely, certainly; for it is twenty-five miles from land, and must be frequently quite shut in by fog and storm. Now come to the other side of the house, and I will show you Katahdin, one hundred and thirty miles away, and perhaps Mount Washington, at a distance of one hundred and seventy. I saw it just now."

So Miselle obediently went, saw all the lions, and then wandered away with the sweet-faced Quakeress to a little nook, where, with the world before them, they enjoyed themselves in a desultory feminine fashion, careless of names or distances, but vividly conscious of every point of beauty in sky or sea or land.

"I think this will do us good for the whole year—don't thee?" asked Miselle's companion; and out of a full heart she could answer only "Yes."

Then came "the world's people," joyous and noisy, and Miselle retraced the few steps she had reverently taken into the pure, sweet chambers of that saintly life, and joined in Chibiabos's merry chorus, and emulated Atalanta's daring leaps from point to point of the rocky path leading to the brow of the ravine—a precipitous cleft between Green Mountain and its easterly spur sometimes called Dry Mountain. Beyond this again lies Newport Mountain, and then the sea. The Green Mountain, or eastern face of this ravine, is composed of bare, storm-scattered rock, and so precipitous that a stone launched from the summit drops a thousand feet to the valley below, striking fire from a dozen salient points of the precipice as it goes, and announcing the end of its journey by a faint and distant crash, while a curious double echo repeats the sound of its fall—first from Otter Creek to the west; and some seconds later from some point far to the east, apparently the open sea.

"Probably our friends the Titans came here to repose in the 'lap of Nature,' " suggested the Count. "Fancy one of them resting his head upon the breast of Dry Mountain, and his body in the wooded valley below, while his feet dabbled luxuriously in the waters of Otter Creek."

Here Caleb launched a fragment of rock so large that its thunderous descent aroused the eagles who inhabit Newport, and who now rose, screaming angrily, from their eyrie.

"Nine of them, as I'm a sinner!" exclaimed Caleb, in great excitement.

And Miselle remarked to Atalanta, "How fortunate we are not chickens, or even lambs!"

"Don't be afraid; those gentlemen have, or soon will have, other fish than you to fry," remarked Caleb; while the Ambassador, always practical, proclaimed his discovery of a nook filled with the largest blueberries ever seen.

"There is a lively sympathy between us and the lower animals after all. They are always grubbing 'round for something to eat, and so are we," suggested Atalanta, meditatively plucking the blueberries.

And so home again.

The next day the gentlemen, headed by the General, devoted to a fishing excursion; and their disconsolate relicts, left to themselves, also hired a roomy rowboat with the two sturdy mariners appertaining, and set forth upon a voyage to the Ovens, an unromantic name given to certain curious caves worn by action of the tide in the base of certain picturesque crags upon the shore of Saulsbury Cove.

"Ovens!" exclaimed Mrs. General indignantly, as the party strolled along the beach, looking up at the bold cliffs toppling above their heads, their wide seams green with ferns and blue with harebells, while from the crest nodded birch and larch, and many another graceful growth—"Ovens indeed! This place is henceforth to be called Saulsbury Crags."

"It is a vote," announced the Speaker; and Miselle "resp'y submit" the idea.

The day was charming, so was the company, so was the lunch, eaten in the largest oven, so was the row homeward, so was the evening, when the fishermen returned wet and dirty beyond belief, hungry, boastful, and happy beyond expression.

The next day was devoted to "the long drive," a tour embracing the village of Seal Cove, Northeast Harbor, and Somesville, a curious seawall or natural causeway composed of pebbles, thrown up by the ocean, but not equal to a similar formation at the other side of Somes Sound, near Southwest Harbor.

But the limits of a magazine paper are peremptory, and by no means admit narrations of all the wonderful adventures that befell the party in this expedition, of how they lost their way, and were fain to send out an exploring expedition; of how they sought shelter and advice in Rhoda Wasgott's Variety Store at Seal Cove, and were referred to a friendly farmhouse close at hand, where they received kindest hospitality, much new milk, bread, butter, doughnuts, and apple pie, and where, to Miselle's rapturous delight, she found a woman spinning real bona fide yarn to be knitted into stockings, and learned, furthermore, that the dwellers in this primitive region still spin and weave and wear the wool of their own sheep, precisely as all our grandmothers once did.

From these scanty "specimen bricks" let the reader build up for himself the story of a long and charming day, ending in a rattling drive homeward, and an impromptu concert at "the other house."

The following morning was devoted to a scramble up a perpendicular mountain for the purpose of obtaining what Atalanta recommended as a "tidy little view"; and Miselle, mentally adjusting the price of candles to the pleasure of such a game, declined accompanying her friends farther than a cottage at the foot of the mountain, where she begged hospitality until their return. It was granted with ready kindness; and while the hostess continued her washing, Miselle devoted herself to a large rocking chair, a little girl named Aqua, and a new field of observation.

"You don't feel the storms here as they do on the coast, do you?" asked she, looking out at the surrounding mountains.

"No, it's an awful sight lee-er here under the hills than right out on shore, you see; but then it's dretful lonesome come to die here in the winter, and a man have to go eight mile a-horseback through the mountains' fore he can fetch a doctor, and you mebbe gone 'fore he gets back."

It was a handful out of her inmost heart that the woman thus gave, and Miselle glanced with sudden appreciation at her hollow cheeks and over-bright eyes.

Presently the hostess, wiping her arms, and, sending Anselm for "kin'lins," busied herself over the stove for a few minutes, and returned with a steaming cup of tea and a cup of milk.

"Thought mebbe you'd take a dish o' tea along o' me," said she. "You don't look so dretful rugged; and it'll kind o' rest ye."

And Miselle, sipping the tea, thought of certain holy words: "For all they did cast in of their abundance, but she of her want did cast in all that she had, even all her living."

Before the lunch was ended, the mountaineers returned, as footsore, ragged, tired, and cross as they deserved to be, and Miselle bid good-bye to her new friend with real regret.

"We are all invited to a *bal masque* at the Bayview House this evening," announced Atalanta at dinner, "and we are all going, which is more."

So the afternoon was devoted to finery and contrivance; the early evening to dressing a Benedictine monk, a Calcutta baboo, and a gypsy fortune-teller; and the first hours of the night to dancing and nonsense.

"The moon knows better than to go to masquerades; she stays out of doors, and enjoys herself like a rational creature," said Miselle, between two yawns, as she walked home.

"You should have been a monk and shrived pretty penitents," said Caleb, laughing with much apparent satisfaction.

But, *Halte-là*! cries the editorial voice, and Miselle pauses, saying, with the wily Scheherezade, "However curious these things may be, what I have yet to tell will divert you infinitely more."

"Pooh!" growls the philosopher. "Because you like a thing, why expect all the world to like it also? How many unfortunate tourists now may be beguiled into visiting it only to find that your swans are geese, and to come away railing at your rose-colored delusions."

"The swans may be geese, and the eagles carrion crows," serenely replied Miselle; "but the larks of Mount Desert are not to be doubted, for Caleb found one there, and it did him a world of good."

Jane G. Austin (1831–1894)

Jane Goodwin Austin was born in Worcester, Massachusetts, to a family that descended from the Pilgrims of Plymouth Rock. Her brother, John A. Goodwin, was a United States congressman and Speaker of the House. When she was a young girl her family moved to Boston where she was educated in private schools. After her marriage to Loring Henry Austin, she moved with her husband to Concord, Massachusetts. There she wrote over two dozen novels and collections of short stories, many of which celebrated the heroism of her Pilgrim ancestry. She developed a close friendship with Louisa May Alcott (to whom she dedicated her book, Cipher*), and her Concord literary associates also included Ralph Waldo Emerson and Nathaniel Hawthorne.*

Chapter 2

Under the Sea

Susan Coolidge (Sarah Chauncey Woolsey)
1876

A melodramatic story set in the Ovens, a once popular tourist site on Mount Desert, demonstrating both the danger of the tides and the deplorable attitude toward the island's native population. "Under the Sea" was one of several stories in the author's collection, For Summer Afternoons *(Boston: Roberts Brothers, 1876).*

They were scrambling down the rocks, a gay, chattering procession—pretty Kate with her captain; Dr. Gray supporting his invalid wife; Helen, Isabel, Tom, and their midshipman cousin; last of all, Esther Vane—alone. It seemed to her morbid fancy right that it should be so. Henceforth she must be alone—always.

The little guide trotted on in advance—his round, ten-year-old face wearing the vacant look so strangely common to that part of the Maine coast, with its glorious scenery. There the ocean is considered simply a vast depot of herrings and "porgy-oil," and the mountains as untoward obstacles in the way of a primitive husbandry. "Blast 'em, I wish they was flat," the natives say, as their ploughs encounter the boulders at the base; and, if they look aloft at all, it is to calculate the perches of "medder land" which might be made to occupy the same area, if the heights were out of the way.

Our party felt on the eve of great things. Having arrived only the day before, Mount Newport with its wonderful reach of sapphire sea, the bluffs, the lakes in their settings of dark-blue hill, were still to them the images of things not seen. This, their first excursion, they had dedicated to the "Grotto," or "Devil's Oven," as the coast people term it; a sort of submarine cave, unveiled and accessible at low tide only, and a great wonder in its way.

The path grew steeper. Carefully they followed its windings, step by step, surefooted Kate accepting the help she didn't need, for that pleasure in being guided and watched. And now the little guide pauses, and with a freckled forefinger points 'round a projection of rock. All crowd to the spot. Ah! there it is!—the cave of the mermaids! A shriek of mingled surprise and enchantment burst from the party at the sight.

Beneath the low-browed arch the rocky floor rose, terrace after terrace, till in its highest recess it met the roof above. A floor for the nereids to dance upon; a floor of pink coralline, gleaming here and there through pools of emerald water left by the retreating tide. And each of these tiny lakelets seemed brimming with flowers—the flowers of ocean—green whorls, like chestnut burs; anemones with their dahlia bloom; brown and rosy mosses among whose tendrils bright fish darted and played, and snails of vivid orange clustered; broad leaves of brilliant dye swaying and undulating with the motion of the pool—minute specks of life flashing every iridescent hue; earthly garden was never so gorgeous. The rocky shelves were dimpled with hollows—softly, exquisitely curved. No fancy of the old classic days seemed too fantastic or too fair for the spot. The imagination instinctively kindled into pictures, and saw the sea nymphs sporting in the foam; bold tritons winding their shells; mermaids playing at hide-and-seek; nixies and mocking watersprites peeping from the basins— all dreamland and wonderland opening, and the common earth put aside and far away.

With cries of delight the party made their way down, and scattered through the cave. There was room for an army. It was hard to realize that with the returning tide the space must fill, the gateway close, and leave no resting place for human foot.

"You said the tide was going down, didn't you, little boy?"

"Ye-ah."

"You're sure?"

"Ye-ah."

"That's nice," cried Isabel. "Then we can stay as long as we like. Oh! Do somebody come here and see this."

She was lying with her face almost touching the anemones. Nobody responded to her call—each had found some other point of interest. Tom had fished up a sea urchin and was exhibiting it. Kate and the captain, in a niche of their own, at safe whispering distance, were absorbed in each other. Esther had climbed to the topmost ledge, and was sitting there alone. For the first time in six weary months a sensation of pleasure had come to her, and she was conscious of but one longing—that they would all go away and leave her to realize it. With some vague hope she got out color box and portfolio, and began to sketch. Sketching she had discovered kept people off, and furnished an excuse for silence.

And so an hour or more passed by. She heard, as in a dream, the chatter of the others, their questions to the little guide, his short, jerky replies. The pools were all explored; the urchins and anemones had been tickled with parasols, and made to shut and open and shut again; the young people began to sigh for further worlds to conquer, and Mrs. Gray to consider it very damp.

"Little boy, isn't there something else nearby which we should like to see?"

"Guess so."

"Well, what is it? Tell us, please."

"There's the 'Heads,' I guess."

"Oh! How far oft is that? A mile, did you say? That's not far. Papa, the boy says there's a place called the 'Heads,' only a mile away, and we want to go and see it. Can't we go? You know the way, don't you, little boy?"

"Ye-ah."

"I think *this* place is very damp," sighed Mrs. Gray. "I should really be glad to go somewhere and feel the sunshine again. I begin to have creeping chills. Suppose we let the boy show us the way to this other place, Father."

"Very well. Get your things together, girls. Come, Esther, we're going."

Esther roused herself as from a dream. "Oh Mr. Gray! Must I go? I'm in the middle of a sketch, you see. Couldn't you leave me here quietly, and pick me up as you come back? I should like it so much."

"Well—I don't know. The tide is going out, the boy says; there won't be any trouble of that kind. Are you sure you won't be chilled or lonely?"

"Oh! Quite sure."

"Promise me that if you are, you will go to the cottage at the bend and warm yourself, or sit on the rocks in the sun. We'll look for you in one place or the other. Good-bye, my dear."

"Good-bye, sir."

"And, oh Esther! You must have some lunch. You'll be starved before we come back," cried careful Helen. So she and Tom and a basket made their way upward, and a deposit of sandwiches and port wine was left in a convenient crevice within reach.

"Good-bye, dear. I hope the sketch will be lovely." And they were gone—up the cliff side—Mrs. Gray last, leaning upon her husband's arm.

"Poor child," she said, "it makes my heart ache to see her look so sad. Didn't you notice how she was longing to have us go, and leave her alone? "

"And the very worst thing for her. She needs rousing, and all this morbid thinking does her harm."

The voices died away. Esther caught the words, and she smiled at them—a bitter little smile. That was what all of them had said since her trouble came. She must be roused, amused—and they had crowded business and pleasure upon her until she sometimes felt that she could bear it no longer. This was the first time in many weeks that she had felt really free—free to be silent, to look sad, to cry if she wished. What a luxury it was! No anxious-eyed mother to watch her—these comparative strangers withdrawn—this cool, darkling silence—it was delicious! There was something in the very nature of her trial which made it necessary to veil her grief with reserve. A black dress she might wear—Paul was a cousin, and some show of mourning is allowed for second cousinhood even, and for intimate friendship such as theirs had been. But no one knew of the unavowed engagement which bound them since that hurried farewell letter in which his love found utterance, and which only reached her after he sailed—the sailing from which there was to be no return. No one knew, as they talked compassionately of her having had a "dreadful shock, poor girl—her own cousin, you know, and such a fine young fellow,"—that her heart was wearing widow's weeds, and mourning its dead as the great loss of life. It wouldn't bear talking about, so she kept silence, and tried to wear a brave face.

At first there had been a little hope as rumors came of one boatload escaping from the midnight collision; but that was over now, and the terrible suspense of hope was over, and every tiling had faded into a sort of gray acceptance of sorrow. The light had gone out.

Left alone, she found with some surprise that she didn't want to cry. All the morning she had felt that to creep away somewhere and weep and weep her heart out would be so good; but tears are contrary things. She sat there dulled into a calm that was almost like content. She was thinking of the time when Paul had visited the island and climbed about that very cave. On the very rock shelf where she sat he might perhaps have rested. She liked to think so. It brought him nearer.

A little later, she put her sketch away and crept down to a broad ledge, where, through the arch, the exquisite skyline was visible. The surf tumbled, and chimed like distant bells. She lay as if fascinated, her eyes fixed upon the shining horizon. Somewhere far beyond it was the spot where the good ship which held her all went down. Down where? Her imagination ran riot. Cleaving the liquid depths to the inmost sanctuary of ocean, she saw the golden sands, the shadowy green light percolating through miles of water—the everlasting repose which reigned there beyond the reach of storm, wind, or hurricane. She tried to fix the wandering images, and to think of it as a haven no less tranquil than the quiet mounds under which are pillowed beloved heads on earth. But it would not stay. Thoughts of tempest and fury, of chill piping winds whipping the foam from the waves, of roar and tumult, and a heaving wilderness of dark waters, came over her, and through all the refrain of Jean Ingelow's pathetic strain mixed and blended:

> "And I shall see thee no more, no more,
> Till the sea gives up its dead."

Great drops forced themselves beneath the closed eyelids, and she sobbed: "Oh Paul, Paul! How can I bear it?"

And then she thought, as she had thought before, how glad she should be to die! Life didn't seem desirable any longer, and it would be blessed to be with Paul, even at the bottom of the ocean. And, thinking thus, the long eyelashes drooped more and more heavily, peace fell upon the brow and lips: she was asleep, asleep, and dreaming a sweet joyful dream.

How long she slept she never knew. She awoke with a sensation of intense cold. The spell of slumber was so strong upon her that for a moment she did not realize what had taken place. The cave was half full of water. Her feet and the hem of her dress were already wet, and the roar of the waves beneath the hardly distinguishable archway told that the tide had surprised another victim, and already the avenue of escape was barred.

Was this the answer to some unspoken prayer?

The thought flashed over her. Had she really prayed for death? Here it was, close at hand, and she was conscious of no gladness—only an intense instinctive desire for life. It was too dreadful to be drowned in that hole, and washed away like a weed. Life was worth living, after all.

Had somebody said, or was she dreaming, that a portion of the cave was left uncovered by the water? She could not remember, but now she searched about for some indication. Ah! Surely, this was one: a cork, a scrap of paper, lodged on the highest shelf, fragile things which a tide must inevitably have washed away. With that instinct of property which survives shipwreck and fire, she collected her drawing materials and other little belongings, and retreating with them to this possible place of refuge, wrapped her cloak about her, and with folded hands sat down to await her fate.

The cave was full of pale green light. It was beautiful to see, as the advancing flow rose ledge over ledge and flooded the fairy pools, how each starflower and sea urchin, each crimson and golden weed, trembled and quivered as with delight at its refreshing touch. Each anemone threw wide its petals and expanded into full blossom to meet the spray baptism. No mortal eye ever looked upon sight more charming; but its beauty was lost to the shivering and terrified girl.

The doorway had quite disappeared. Sharp spray dashed against her dress. The drops struck her face. She shrank, and clung more tightly to the rock. A prayer rose to her lips; and through the tremulous light of the submerged archway a strange shadow began to go and come, to move and pause, and move again. Was it fish, or weed, or some mysterious presence? Did it come accompanied by life or death?

Meantime upon the rocks above a distracted group were collected. The party had come gaily back from the "Heads." Dr. Gray, ignorant landsman as he was, had grown uneasy and hurried them away. Arrived at the "Grotto," the full extent of the calamity was at once evident. The boy had mistaken the tide—flow for ebb—and the only hope left was that Esther, discovering her danger in time, had taken refuge at the cottage nearby. Thither they flew to search; but, as we know, in vain.

The sobbing girls hung distractedly over the cliff, listening to the hollow boom with which the waves swung into the cavern beneath—sickening to think of the awful something which might any moment wash outward on the returning billow. The gentlemen went for assistance, and brought a couple of stout fishermen to the spot. But what could anybody do?

"If the young woman has sense enough to climb up the right-hand corner and set still, it won't hurt her none perhaps," one of them said.

"Not more nor two tides a year gets up there." Ah! If Esther could only be told that! They could but trust powerlessly to her steadiness of nerve and common sense.

"She's such a wise thing," Helen sobbed out. So they waited.

A rattle of wheels came from the road. They all turned to look, and someone said: "Perhaps it's a doctor!" Though what earthly use a doctor could have been would be hard to say!

A figure was coming rapidly up the path, a young man. Nobody recognized him, till Dr. Gray started forward with the face of one who sees a ghost.

"Paul! Good God! Is it possible?"

"Yes, Doctor," with a hasty handshake. "No other. I don't wonder you stare."

"But, in heaven's name, how has it come about? Where have you been since we gave you up for lost?"

"It's a long story. You shall hear it someday. But"—rapidly—"forgive my impatience—where is my cousin? What is the matter?"

There was a dead silence. At last, with a groan, Dr. Gray spoke:

"Paul, my poor fellow, how can I tell you! Esther is below there."

"In the 'Grotto'?"

"In the 'Grotto.' Can anything be done?"

The young man staggered. The glow faded from his face, leaving him ashy pale. For a moment he stood irresolute, then he roused himself, and his voice though husky was firm: "It's a frightful place; still there is no absolute danger if she keeps her presence of mind. I stayed there over a tide myself once, just to see it. Is your boat at home?" to one of the fishermen.

"Yes, sir."

"Fetch it 'round then as quickly as possible." Then to Dr. Gray: "I shall row out there opposite the entrance, and make a dive for it. If I come up inside, it's all right, and I'll see that no harm happens to Esther till the water falls, and we can get her out."

"But—the risk!"

"There is the risk of striking the arch as I rise—that is all. I'm a good swimmer, Doctor, as you know. I think it can be done. You can guess," with a sort of pale smile, "how I have been counting on this meeting; and to leave her alone and frightened, and not go to her, is just impossible. I shall manage it—never fear."

The boat came. They saw it rowed out—Paul taking the bearings carefully, shifting position once, and yet again, before satisfied. Then he looked up with bright, confident eyes and a nod, and clasped his hands above his head. A splash—he was gone, and the water closed over him.

Within the cave, Esther watched the strange, moving phantom which darkened the entrance. The splash reached without startling her, but in another second a flashing object whirled down and inward, and, rising, the waves revealed a face—a white face with wet hair. In the pale, unearthly glow, it wore the aspect of death. It drew nearer: she covered her eyes with her hands. Was the sea giving up its dead, that here, in this fearful solitude, the vision of her drowned Paul confronted her—or was she going mad?

Another second, and the hands were withdrawn. The peril, the excitement of the past hour, the strangeness and unreality of the spot, combined to kindle within her an unnatural exaltation of feeling. Had she not craved this? If they met as spirits in this land of spirits, was she to be afraid of Paul or shrink from him? No, a thousand times no!

The face was close upon her. With rapid strokes, it drew near—a form emerged—it was upon the rocks. With a shriek, she held out her arms. Cold hands clasped hers—a voice (did dead men speak?) cried: "Queenie, Queenie!"

The old pet name! It was Paul's ghost, but none the less Paul. "I know you are dead," she said, "but I am not afraid of you," and felt, unterrified, a strong arm enfold her. But the breast upon which her cheek rested was throbbing with such living pulsations that, half aroused, she began to shudder in a terrible blended hope and fear, and she shrank away from his touch.

"Oh Paul! Are we both dead, or only you? Is this the other world?"

"Why, darling," gently seating her on the rock, "you are in a dream. Wake up, love. Look at me, Esther. I am not a dead man, but your living Paul. Feel my hand—it is warm, you see. God has restored us to one another; and now, if His mercy permits, we will never be parted again."

"Paul! Paul!" cried Esther, convinced at last.

They were very happy. Prosy folk, could they have looked in, would have seen only two exceedingly wet young persons seated high up on a rocky ledge, with receding waters rippling about their feet; but they, all aglow with life and happiness, scarcely knew of the lapse of time before the shimmering line of light appeared at the mouth of the cave.

With blessed tears streaming down her cheeks, Esther heard his story; how, picked up—the sole survivor of that dreadful wreck—by an India-bound trader, her lover had lain delirious for many weeks in a far land, unable to tell his name or story; and, in part recovered, started at once for home, and landed in advance of the letters which told his safety. And so they had met here, 'mid "coral and tangle and almoridine"; and, as she heard the history of his perils, Esther clasped the hand she held as if she never again could let it go.

That provident little Helen—bless her heart!—"builded better than she knew," in providing such a store of damp sandwiches and refreshing wine for those drenched and happy lovers. And when at last the receding tide opened again the rocky gate and the vista of the sea tinged with rosy sunset, and Esther, aided by strong arms, left her prison, it was with a glow like the sunset upon her cheeks, and in her eyes such a radiance of happiness that it fairly dazzled the forlorn, bedraggled group above. Mrs. Gray embraced her fondly, and fell incontinently into a fit of long-deferred hysterics. The boys executed a war dance of congratulation, and Helen and Isabel laughed and cried for joy. And as Esther turned with Paul for a last look at the scene of her deliverance, the chime and murmur of the sea seemed full of blessing—the blessing of the dear Lord who had had compassion upon her weakness, restoring her to life, and to that life its lost joy. With thankful heart, she went her way.

So we leave her.

***Susan Coolidge** (1835–1905)*

Susan Coolidge was the pseudonym of Sarah Chauncey Woolsey, born in Cleveland, Ohio, into a family related to John Winthrop, the first governor of the Massachusetts Bay Colony; Jonathan Edwards, the famed eighteenth century theologian and philosopher; and also to three presidents of Yale, Timothy Dwight, Theodore Dwight Woolsey, and Timothy Dwight Jr. After private schooling in Cleveland and boarding school studies in New Hampshire, she moved to New Haven, Connecticut, where she lived for fifteen years. After two years in Europe she settled in Newport, Rhode Island. Under her pen name, she also composed many poems and children's books.

Chapter 3

Oxygen! A Mt. Desert Pastoral

Robert Grant
1879

In his autobiography, the author described the American woman in this play as "a goddess for whom nothing was too good and with whom no liberties could be taken." It was so easy for him to describe this tale of "idyllic innocence" that the "words flowed from [his] pen" even though he never personally set foot on Mount Desert Island. This play originally appeared in the Harvard Lampoon *and then was included in the author's* Little Tin Gods-on-Wheels: or, Society in our Modern Athens, a Trilogy After the Manner of the Greeks *(Cambridge, Mass.: Charles W. Sever, 1879).*

***

A trifle offered by Lampy without comment, as an example of the effect that a bracing atmosphere can produce upon conservative natures.

DRAMATIS PERSONÆ

MISS ALICE BUNTING, *of Philadelphia, ætatis 21 yrs. 6 mos.*
MR. ARTHUR FLANNELSHIRT, *A. B., LL. B., of Boston, ætatis 26 yrs. 3 mos.*

SCENE I.—*Mt. Desert. Corridor of Rodick House.*
Hour, 10:30 P.M.

Enter MISS BUNTING *and* MR. FLANNELSHIRT *arm in arm. Her dress is a blue and white boating-suit, cut short. A hat with a huge brim and draped with a large red handkerchief is perched on the back of her hand. He is attired in a gray shirt of flannel, a pair of patched pantaloons, a skullcap, and canvas shoes. He is smoking a pipe. She pauses at room twenty, and taking a key from her pocket gives it to him. He unlocks the door. She goes in and returns with a small pitcher.*

ALICE.

And now, good night. But ere you go, do get me,
as usual, some hot water from the kitchen.

ARTHUR.

Give me the jug, and in half a jiffy
I will be back. *(Runs down the corridor.)*

ALICE *(shrieking after him).*

Be sure that it is boiling!

She goes into her room and shuts the door. Interval of five minutes. Re-enter Arthur, with the pitcher of hot water and a plate of hard crackers. He knocks, and she puts her head out.

ALICE.

What made you take so long? But oh, how lovely,
to bring me some hard crackers too! Just toss me
one from the plate and see if I can catch it.

He does so, and she, emerging from the room, tries to catch it in her mouth. The cracker falls on the ground. They both stoop to pick up the pieces, and bump their heads.

ALICE.

You horrid thing! You stupid, awkward creature!

She playfully flings the bits of cracker at him.

ARTHUR.

Come now, it's much too early to retire.
Let's go and eat our crackers on the staircase;
it would be sort of weird. Say, don't you think so?

ALICE.

Why, yes. I think it would be quite romantic!
You really can't imagine what a comfort
it is to have no matron to annoy one,
to dog one's steps and harp on what is proper!
A girl that's civilized don't need a matron.
Thank heaven, Father let me come without one.
He kicked at first, but by judicious treatment
I brought him 'round. I'm ready now, if you are.

They proceed to the staircase and sit down on the top stair, with the water pitcher between them.

ALICE *(munching crackers).*

Oh, ain't this jolly, it is so informal!
Why, only think, we two set out together

at nine this morning to explore and ramble.
We've spent the day together on the mountain,
and never parted once. The heat of noontide
found us companions still, and evening's shadow
saw you and me without a person near us.
Where else, but here, could we do this without
exciting comment?

ARTHUR.

Nowhere, sad to mention.
In Boston, where I live, if I should happen
to walk twice with some fascinating creature
I should dead certain be reported smitten,
engaged, and when that turned out false, rejected.
But here, to pass the day with whom you want to,
pass two days, three days, four days, even five days,
in the society of girls one fancies,
is not regarded as the least peculiar.
What do you say, now, to a row by moonlight?

ALICE.

The very thing! Oh, what a boon is freedom!

They rise from the stairs. She goes to her room and gets a shawl, which he tenderly puts over her shoulders. Arm in arm they go down, leaving the pitcher in the middle of the staircase.

SCENE II.—*Bar Harbor. Mt. Desert.*

A rowboat is floating on the tranquil water. A nearly full moon is high in the heavens. She is stretched out in the stern. He slowly paddles with the oars. Several other boats can be seen in the distance, but not near enough to distinguish the parties.

ALICE.

This is a first-rate place to get acquainted;
day before yesterday I'd never seen you,
and now I feel as if I'd known you ages.

ARTHUR.

In my prim city, I might live next door to
a girl for ten years, and not know her nearly
as well as I know you. This comes of freedom!
Look at those boats on this side and on that side,
each freighted with two other kindred spirits,
More intimate, perhaps, than even we are.
They probably have rambled weeks together,
and rowed upon the water every evening.
This beats the New Republic all to hollow;
Paul and Virginia were nothing to it.

ALICE.

If I were at Nahant, Cohasset, Newport,
or any other of those horrid places,
I should be forced in cold blood to abandon
this blessed moon, and go to bed when Pa did.
But, fortunately, Mrs. Easy-Going,
who promised Pa to keep an eye on me,
don't care a button what I do, provided

I do not interfere with her Amelia,
who spends her time with little Peter Minestock.
I hope she'll get him, but I pity Peter!

By way of variety, she gives him a playful splatter with the oar. He laughs, and splatters her back. He proposes to anchor, and she acquiesces. She stretches herself out in the stern, he in the bow, with a pipe.

ALICE.

Now, ain't this lovely, to be so devoted!
It's twenty times as good as an engagement,
because we know that, if we ever happen
to weary of each other, we have only
to part, and cotton to another person,
you to some girl, and I to some new fellow.

ARTHUR.

I could spend years with you and never weary!

ALICE.

Don't be too sure. You're merely a spring chicken,
and I have practiced this thing four summers.
You will get sick of me before a fortnight
is ended.

ARTHUR.

Never, oh, believe me, never;
I ne'er have seen a girl that I admired,
adored, respected, loved, and venerated
so much as I do you.

ALICE.

What perfect nonsense!
What would your ma say? Oh, young man, be careful;
all Philadelphians are not like me, sir!
Nine out of ten would snap you up directly
for words like those, and marry you before you
could count Jack Robinson!

ARTHUR.

Oh lovely being!
I'm thine forever, if you only say so.
For all I care, my ma may go to glory.

ALICE.

How sweet to be thus loved! No more at present,
I will reflect on what you say. It's time now
to go to bed. What hour says your repeater?

ARTHUR.

'Tis half past twelve.

ALICE.

'Tis sad to part, but needful.

They slowly get to rights and haul up the anchor. She takes the oars and rows toward the shore; he puffs his pipe pensively.

SCENE III.—*Mt. Desert. Corridor of Rodick House.*
Hour, 1:15 A.M.

They reenter arm-in-arm. Somebody has stepped on and upset the pitcher during their absence. After a few minutes' conversation he goes and gets some more boiling water.

ALICE *(going into her room).*

And now, once more, good night.

ARTHUR.

Tomorrow morning
I'll come at nine.

ALICE *(sticking her head out).*

All right, I shall be ready,
and we will spend the day again together,
as usual to our mutual satisfaction.
We'll climb, read poetry, drive, row, loaf, and ramble
from morn to dewy eve, and I will teach you
the latest dodge in scientific flirting;
giving you points, and Heaven knows you need them!
You'll be an adept by this time next summer,
if you don't let such stuffs as that you uttered
tonight destroy the fruits of my good teaching.
But when, in future days, you are distinguished
for being able with your little finger
to set the heart of any girl a beating,
and not care a rush, say that I taught you.
Say, "Alice Bunting, a sweet Philadelphian,
a maiden unaffected and spontaneous,
who always did exactly what she wanted,

and went from principle without a matron,
found me a callow youth, a perfect chicken,
and made me what I am. Be hers the glory."
Good night, good night! Remember, nine tomorrow.

Kisses her hand to him, and closes the door.

ARTHUR.

Good night, good night! Oh, why ain't more girls like her!

Walks slowly and pensively down the corridor.

***Robert Grant** (1852–1940)*

Robert Grant was a Boston native, educated at Boston Latin School, after which he earned three degrees from Harvard University. He went on to practice law and eventually served as a probate judge in Boston, while writing several novels and light verse. He was a frequent contributor to the Harvard Lampoon.

Chapter 4

A Midsummer-Night's Adventure

Anna Bowman Blake

1880

Like many Bar Harbor tales, this story of flirtation encounters a dangerous episode, and along the way captures the character and culture of the "discovered, the appropriated, the fashionable Mount Desert." Though our hero regrets that "the wilderness was a wilderness no longer," he finds compensation in the "charming girls and the handsome women in irreproachable French toilets." This story appeared in Harper's New Monthly Magazine, *vol. 61, issue 364 (September 1880).*

"It's abominable! It's outrageous! There isn't a thing on the table fit for a decent man to eat. The cook ought to be put to death. Hanging would be too good for her for I'll be bound it's a woman; no man would have the effrontery to send up such disgraceful stuff. She ought to be strangled, and with her own food. Bah! That dreadful breakfast is sticking in my throat yet."

The above-uttered words, spoken with vehement emphasis of irritability, were accompanied by an energetic pushing aside of the various platters of leathery beef, underdone potatoes, and bullet-headed peas. For Mr. Hugh Wilder had arrived at an age and to proportions of rotundity when a man takes serious views of the dinner question. No wonder, then, that he found himself wholly unable to accept in the true spirit of resignation the scant accommodation in edibles offered the Mount Desert summer boarder.

"Heavens!" he was continuing, preparing to fire off another volley of disgust, "I shall die of indigestion if I stay here another week."

"But you know you *would* come," bleated a lady by this protesting gentleman's side, softly and inoffensively, as if fearing to excite him the more. She was presumably his wife, if one were only to infer such a conclusion from the general rule governing the matrimonial choice. She belonged to him by every law of contrast. She looked as mild as he was explosive, as bleached as he was highly colored, and had the air of being one of those marital moons that only shine by reflected light. A close observer might have discovered that the moral atmosphere of this moonlit character was of a depressingly exhausted nature. There was a hopeless look of resignation emitted through the medium of her pale blue eye. She had an extinguished air, as if her previous efforts to throw cold water on the volcanic ebullitions of her lord had, so to speak, worn her out. She was administering now a feebly repressive glance, that carried no hope of success in it.

"Would come," the explosive gentleman replied, echoing her words. "Do you suppose I expected this?" with a comprehensive sweep of his fork over the half-cooked food before him. "I supposed at least we should be able to live like Christians; but a Turk couldn't stand this. Pie, do you say?"—to the waitress, who was passing him various specimens of that truly characteristic American pastry. "Yes, I'll take some pie. It's the only good thing there is here. Some mince, please. One is sure of getting at least a bit of meat—and cooked—in a mince pie. Coffee? No, thank you. We make our own. There's where we showed a grain of wisdom. Violet"—turning to a young lady at his left—"send for the hot water, will you? Drink their coffee! It's the most infernal—"

"Uncle!" exclaimed the young girl addressed as Violet, in a tone of commanding remonstrance a tone singularly soft, and of control to richness. For all its softness, her single word produced its effect. The volcano was extinguished, and Mr. Wilder continued to eat his repast in silence; with something, it is true, of that dejected air a man wears who has been successfully snubbed into silence by two women.

This little domestic episode had served as the *sauce piquante* to the midday meal of a certain light-haired young gentleman who sat a few seats removed from the Wilder party. Mr. Rutherford Payson had, indeed, been so thoroughly entertained with the lively play of the gentleman's ill humor, the elder lady's look of uneasy, helpless irritation, and the young girl's air of composed disapproval, that he had quite forgotten to grumble on his own account.

Upon seating himself at the table his eyes had naturally wandered to this party, Miss Violet's attractions being, indeed, of an order to make her the focal point of observation. She was handsome rather than pretty, of the richly colored, abundant-tressed type. It was the sort of beauty which made a little show of anger wonderfully becoming; that hint of indignation had lent a smothered fire of splendor to the dark deep eye; and to the rich chestnut hue of the cheek was added a color which made it wear the ripe, fruity, luscious bloom which so delights the eye in a van Dyck canvas. The young girl's efforts to maintain an air of serene self-control made her square a little defiantly a pair of finely turned shoulders, and gave to her charming round head, with its masses of low-looped hair, a bird-like erectness. Altogether, Payson felt that the moment of observation had been a singularly fortuitous one. A closer observation revealed to Payson that the other features of the face were not up to the scale of beauty attained by the expressive character of her superb eyes. But one could hardly be coldly critical of the faults in the face when one was under the influence of its charm; and the charm was one evoked by the play of sensibility that revealed itself in every changeful expression. This young gentleman was rather given to the interesting pastime of classifying pretty women's faces, and he put Miss Violet's along with those faces that had a soul in them. He suspected she might, upon acquaintance, be found to have a taste for a serious moment.

She was anything but serious now. She was laughing heartily, and making the others laugh. The irascible uncle had lost all traces of his former irritability. He was leading the laughter with trumpet-like blasts of merriment, his anger being, presumably, like the rage of certain beasts of prey, confined to quarreling over his food.

Payson had his own reasons for being thoroughly out of humor with Mount Desert; but his grievances were based on higher grounds than the dismal failures before him in the culinary art.

After a five years' absence abroad, he had returned hoping to find Mount Desert as primitive as he had left it. Fresh from the debris of ruins, there had been bred in him an appetite for the wilderness; and he had caressed his fancy with the hope of finding Mount Desert that charming marriage of mountain and sea still fresh with its perfume of savage sanctity. The very pines, he remembered, had waved with an air of virginal primeval grace. But behold! The wilderness was a wilderness no longer. The place was swarming, not with the flannel-shirted mountaineers, but with myriads of charming girls and handsome women in irreproachable French toilets. The wilderness, indeed, might be said to blossom like the rose, in view of the fact of the number of pretty girls with whom it abounded.

In readjusting his mental focus, Payson was forced to admit he lost nothing in point of amusement. He was conscious of being most delightfully entertained. If America was the country of surprises—indeed, the very genius of the unexpected—his native land certainly yielded compensating stores of pleasure. Mount Desert, the discovered, the appropriated, the fashionable Mount Desert, was only another name for a carnival of pleasure, a Turk's paradise of beauties. Wherever he went, Payson's eyes and ears were greeted with the same sights and sounds. From the caves there came the echo of gay laughter; through the forest there moved the flutter of French gowns. The rocks were made picturesquely alive with vivid, brilliant splashes of color, and a perfectly bewildering maze of loveliness was to be gazed upon at the hops and Germans.

As for the naked little god, he did a most thriving business. Payson had not been many hours on the island before he made the interesting discovery that flirtation, that peculiarly American pastime, was the pivot on which swung all fashionable existence at Mount Desert. Flirtations, indeed, were being carried on in open court, so to speak. This summer operetta seemed to be universally sung in duets; and to a fine ear the active flutter of Monsieur Cupidon's fleet little wings was to be heard in brisk circulation beneath all those widely spread bandanna sunshades, which Payson had come to look upon as an indispensable adjunct to Mount Desert scenery.

To Payson there was something infectious in breathing this air of sentiment. As the days went on he found himself thinking with flattering pertinacity of a certain dark-eyed, brown-haired young woman. And she was no other than the charming Miss Wilder. He was only happy when yielding to the spirit in his feet which led him to become the shadow of her movements. A glimpse of heron on some distant bluff, as she stood, the highlight of a perfect picture, the lines of her figure delightfully defined against the superb blue of sea and sky, the flutter of her scarf—a scarf he had grown to have a fondness for—flying in the breeze of some mountain altitude, were things he was beginning to feed on. Naturally what he longed for was a more substantial diet. But the approaches to knowing her seemed all cut off. They appeared to have no mutual friends. And perhaps the fact that the Wilders came from Boston was sufficient to account for a certain aloofness in their manner. There was, indeed, a touch of New England reserve about them all. Even the expansive uncle seemed awed, when it came to social amenities, by the consciousness that he came from the Hub.

But to Payson, Boston carried no terrors. He had acquired that fine freemasonry of social spirit which comes to a traveled being, and was he to be chilled by a Boston east wind? He recognized no such petty social impediments, and Miss Wilder might be twenty times the haughty Puritan maiden she gave evidence of being, and he would know her.

The following day at dinner he was in the very act of opening fire, when, chancing to look up at Miss Wilder's charming face, an idea—an utterly absurd idea—struck him, and he began to smile. To his confusion, she was returning his look, and for the first time. To his horror, before he could check himself, his smile had broadened, and he was conscious of having very nearly laughed in her face.

He had a vague sense that Miss Wilder's eyes had flashed out at him in mingled surprise and indignation, and that she had colored, and colored deeply, under her perfectly justifiable annoyance. But he had already hastily quitted the table. For the next few moments Mr. Rutherford Payson might have been found at the back door of the hotel apostrophizing the innocent mountains with great fluency of speech—a fluency which rarely comes to a man in trying moments unless he yield to the cheering effects of a discreet profanity.

But he could not have helped it if he had tried. His rudeness had come from an uncontrollable attack of his sense of the ridiculous. That morning on the beach he had fallen into conversation with a native who was busily engaged in shoveling seaweed. Payson fell to wondering how any man could eke out a living on this barren coast. Then he had asked the man how he managed to make a living at all.

"Wa'al, neighbor," the man had answered him, "there bean't nuthin' ter make hereabouts, an' that's a fact. But, yer see, in winter I haul logs, and in summer I haul mealers, and 'twixt the two I dew manage ter squint along." Be it added that in the elegant and realistic vernacular of Mount Desert, the term "mealer" is applied to those boarders living outside in the cottages, for whom, in wet weather, the typical local vehicle, the buckboard, is sent by the hotel-keepers.

When Payson had looked at Miss Wilder's refined, aristocratic turn of feature, and then thought of her as classed under the generic name of "hauled mealer," it had proved too much for him. But at least he could repair his error; he would go and apologize; he would go now.

In his zeal to acquit himself, he rushed toward the piazza. But two ladies, with their arms linked in one another's, blocked the doorway leading to it. As he stood behind them, he caught sight of the profile of one of the ladies. It was that of Miss Wilder's aunt, and she was saying,

"But you thought him so handsome."

And he only too distinctly heard Miss Violet's answer, with its touch of careless disdain: "Which fact doesn't preclude the possibility of his having the worst manners in the world. He is the rudest man I have ever seen." With that, both ladies stepped out, and were soon slowly pacing the long length of the piazza.

Of course, now, he could not have the face to present himself. She had condemned him unheard, and her verdict had been like a blow. All he could do was to keep away. He would see to it that at least she should not even be annoyed by his presence.

Meanwhile he was walking, aimlessly, he hardly knew where. He was conscious only of having as his companions the lively play of his self-reproaches, his futile regrets. He had made a fool of himself—a fact he was communicating with more or less vehemence of utterance to every tree on the roadside. He had made an idiot of himself, and he was taking the very flowers into his confidence. Then with a vicious switch of his cane he would snap off the pretty heads of these innocent offenders, after the fashion of the kings of old, who beheaded a man possessed of too dangerous a secret.

After an hour's walk or so he suddenly determined to turn back. What was the use of wandering about cursing one's folly? He would go back: something might happen. He might meet her, and then who knows? He might find courage to confront her with his excuses and repentance.

As he was sauntering by the wharf, crowded with the usual number of parties about to set off for their afternoon sail, a man whom he knew—Clinton Youngs—rushed hastily past him. Catching sight of Payson, he seized him by the arm, accosting him with: "Just the man! For heaven's sake, help us out, Payson. There isn't an inch of room in one of the boats for that pretty Boston girl, and there isn't a soul to row her over. We're off for the Porcupines. Tea on the rocks, and that sort of thing. It promises to be rather jolly. Come, you must," dragging him along. Before Payson could fairly begin his expostulatory refusal, Clinton Youngs had him confronting the entire party.

"Here's your boat. Do you know the girl—Miss Wilder? No? How awkward! I supposed of course you knew her. She's at your hotel. Miss Wilder, allow me to present Mr. Payson. He insists upon rowing you over by way of making things easier." Payson could have crushed him. "Remember, we're to meet at the Rocks. I must go up for another pair of oars." And Mr. Clinton Youngs was off.

Payson stood still. He felt himself for the moment seized by a kind of masterly indecision. Miss Wilder had only acknowledged his presence by the slightest of slight inclinations: the most ingenious imagination could not call it a bow. Then she had gone on quietly amusing herself with her previous occupation of dabbling with her white fingers in the waters. What should he do? Obey his orders? Or—no! here was his chance, his opportunity. Fate had been kinder to him than his wildest dreams. He was hardly the man to fly now. He had certainly given Miss Wilder time and chance to object to his entering the boat had she so chosen. He had waited a full long moment. But there was no sign, either of consent or dissent, to be read from that down-sweeping glance.

The next instant he had leaped in, and had pushed the boat off. A few vigorous strokes, and they were well out in the bay.

"Miss Wilder," he began, with a kind of desperate directness, after a few seconds of death-like silence—she had not even looked at him yet—"you have every right to think me the rudest man in the world." She blushed at this, slowly raising her eyes. "But won't you suspend a severer judgment until you hear a little story?"

With deliberate frankness he related the history of his morning's adventure, and its tragic consequences. His recital could hardly be called a comic rendering of the situation. He was too terribly in earnest for that. Certain it is that Miss Wilder did not find anything in it to cause her to smile. But when he began to upbraid himself with his dreadful, his inexcusable rudeness, and to tell her how hopeless he felt the situation to be, she smiled radiantly, and answered him, with a delightfully reassuring mockery in her tone:

"Yes, it is hopeless. Perfectly so. Hadn't we better leave it alone? And don't you think, considering we're off on a pleasure jaunt, we ought to try to think of something a little more cheering than our mutual mistakes? Isn't the weather superb? In such a climate one can forgive its mention."

"I suppose Mount Desert is an old story to you?"

"Oh no. We're just being introduced."

"Of course you like it!"

"Oh, it's a paradise—to be young in."

"A paradise, where, it appears, only man is vile," laughingly responded Payson.

"Whose vileness, though, appears to have a saving charm, if one is to believe the evidence of one's senses," brightly retorted the girl. "But," she continued, "I should hate to come here a middle-aged party, shouldn't you? Imagine confronting this sentimental *entourage* with one's worn-out illusions!"

"It would be committing a kind of moral anachronism," answered Payson, sweeping the boat along in easy sculling motion. He was hardly conscious of making any physical exertion to speed their going. He was only delightfully, sentiently stirred with an exhilarating sense of joy and an unwonted elation at carrying away with him over this wide waste of the summer sea so beautiful and charming a girl.

"But where are you going?" she was asking him. "Are you heading right? Aren't you taking us out to sea?"

"You can hardly have the heart to blame me for taking the longest way 'round. I'll turn about, though, if you say so, if you fear the motion of the waves. But this will bring us 'round all right, and we'll have a fine view of the sea."

"I'm not afraid; and it is—oh, isn't it too beautiful!" ejaculated the girl, as she caught her first full glimpse of the open ocean.

But what Payson preferred to look at was the girl herself. She certainly had the art, whether a conscious or an unconscious one, of making pictures for the eyes to delight in. She wore today the hat with the famous veil about it, the veil he had grown to be fond of, and its blue gauze wound 'round her throat was the only touch of color about her. All the rest was white and pale yellow. Her clinging white draperies were gathered loose about her feet and knees, outlining the perfect proportions. In one hand she held a large creamy yellow sunshade, against whose round disk of pale gold the girl's face shone out as shines on certain world-famous canvases the face of a medieval saint with its aureole of glory. Just now the enthusiasm of her delight had kindled the flame of a beautiful moment of emotional flame that lit the face into a glow of ardor. And this girl was no medieval saint, but a breathing woman with a supremely human charm.

Was it any wonder that Payson felt as if he had entered some charmed land that merely to listen to the lapping and beating of the waves was to hear the voices of enchantment?

"But what is that?" suddenly cried the young girl. "See! look! Can it be a cave?" pointing to an opening in the great wall of rock beneath which they were passing. They were under the shadow of the Porcupine Cliff.

"It looks suspiciously like one." Payson rowed his boat farther out into the sea to be safe from the treachery of the rocks.

"Oh, don't go out!" the girl pleaded. "It looks so awfully mysterious and romantic. It looks positively weird. Do go just near enough to see *what* it is."

"I'll cheerfully row you to Chin—but, good heavens! There goes my oar!" As Payson had turned the boat to head in toward the opening, one of his oars, catching between two submerged rocks, had snapped in two. "We're in a pretty fix now."

"And it's all my fault. I'm so sor—"

"My God! We're being sucked in!"

It was true. The great swelling force of the inrushing waters was hurrying their frail bark into the dark cavernous depth. They both had a terrifying sense of the day turning to night, of a vast yawning chasm, of a deafening swash of waters, when the girl suddenly felt herself seized. Clasping her in his arms, Payson had but time for a swift, vigorous spring—a spring which landed them on a projecting ledge of rock and the next instant there was a crash, and their boat was floating past them, dashed into a thousand splintered bits.

"Good heavens! What an escape!" Payson muttered, with a kind of gasp. But neither of them could speak quite yet. It had all been so sudden, the sense of their danger, and the horrible fate from which they had been delivered, that they were stunned for the moment, nerveless and dazed.

Payson was the first to recover himself. He was brought back to acute consciousness by the shivering of the girl beside him. "Are you hurt? Are you cold?" he asked, eagerly.

"No, I'm not hurt; but I believe I am cold. There seems to be water somewhere." She glanced at her feet, over which the incoming waters were breaking every few moments.

"Come, we must go up higher. Give me your hand." He helped her to scale the rocks above them. "This is better. I—I hope you're not going to suffer for this," with an anxious look at her.

"Oh, I'm not a frail being. I shall not catch cold. What I'm wondering at is how we're ever to get out," recovering some of her natural buoyancy, with a comprehensive glance about the great, dark, dismal rocky chamber in which they found themselves.

"The situation does look appalling, I'll allow."

"I suppose there's no chance of our climbing up that cliff?" pointing to the great facade of rock behind them.

"No, it would be impossible. There isn't a foothold anywhere," replied Payson, who had already scanned that loophole of escape with the eye of a practiced Alpine climber. "Miss Wilder, there's no use of holding out to you false hopes. We're in a pretty serious plight. We can't get back by water, since our boat's gone; and we can't climb to the earth's surface, for the rocks are simply unscalable. The only thing we can do is to wait for something to turn up."

"You mean till someone comes after us?"

"I do. And the probabilities are, we shan't be kept waiting long. Our party will soon find us missing, and will begin to look us up. Meanwhile, what can I do to make you comfortable?"

"Nothing, thanks. I'm as comfortable as I feel a right to be under the circumstances."

What a blessing it was she took it all so sensibly! Payson shuddered to think what it would have been with a hysterical young woman on his hands.

"If that's the case, the proper thing for me to do is to make a tour of inspection. My objective point is a pile of driftwood, my intentions a fire, Miss Wilder."

"That's as it should be. We must see to it we do the correct shipwrecked thing."

"Yes, I should hate to feel afterward that we had missed anything." His efforts were rewarded beyond his hopes. He returned with his arms laden with dried seaweed and driftwood. "You see, Miss Wilder, the advantage of having as your fellow comrade an experienced ancient mariner. The sea yields up its treasures to the wise."

"I don't wish to dampen your ardor," returned the girl, demurely, "but have you such a thing as a match about you? Otherwise—"

That was an appalling contingency; but some furious dives into Payson's vestpocket produced *three.* "And I usually am laden down with a bushel," he groaned.

"With good management, we'll make those three do the work of a bushel," encouragingly responded the girl. Wrapping two of them for safekeeping in her handkerchief, Violet faced about, spreading her skirts wide out to protect her from the wind, and struck the remaining match so close to the dry driftwood that at the first spark the little pile was ablaze.

"That was beautifully done. As a shipwrecked mariner you're an enormous success, Miss Wilder."

She laughed, seating herself close to the fire.

"I suppose you know this fire is designed to attract the eye of our discoverer," continued Payson, pointing to the thin wisp of smoke curling upward, which was making its way to heaven through an opening in the rocks just above them. "Seeing that, they'll begin to suspect our whereabouts. At present life has but two duties—the feeding of this fire, and making things as endurable for you as you will let me."

But, indeed, the girl's cheerfulness was robbing the situation of all its objectionable features. Payson, naturally, found the adventure full of a certain charm as well, indeed, it might be, with so admirably pretty and brave a girl as his companion. She met his lively sallies more than halfway. She forestalled him in his attempts to take a humorous view of the affair. With sportive grace she gaily descanted upon the merits of cave scenery, the beauties of rocky elevations, and soliloquized upon the fact of what a really comfortable time witches must have.

"Doesn't it seem to you it's getting very dark?" suddenly asked the girl. "Why, look! The stars are out."

Payson took out his watch. "It's nearly nine, by Jove!"

"And—and they've never come for us. They've—oh, Mr. Payson," cried the girl, starting wildly to her feet, with a ring of distress in her voice, "do you suppose—what if we should have to pass the night here?"

Payson grasped the girl's trembling hands, hoping to calm her. "My dear Miss Wilder, there is no such possibility. Pray sit down, and let's be reasonable. Our friends, when we failed to appear, concluded we had turned back. They are expecting to meet us at the hotel. Failing to find us there, they'll then begin their search. And that smoke, pointing to the circling column, will sufficiently proclaim our dilemma. Before midnight you'll be sleeping quietly in your bed. But, in the meantime, it's getting colder. Here, you must wrap this about you," proceeding to divest himself of his Knickerbocker jacket.

"Mr. Payson, I'll do nothing of the kind. Do you take me for inhuman?"

"I take you to be what you are, a perfectly reasonable young woman. You're about to prove your reasonableness by doing as I say."

"I will never wear it," insistently, with something of the defiant look he had seen on her face the first day.

"But you will. And now, at once. I'm used to being obeyed." He spoke in a tone not to be made light of. She could see the determination flaming in his eye.

"Oh, well, if it's as bad as that. If it's become a habit"—submitting gracefully then to his putting it about her, with a touch of mock submission in her voice.

But she was not wholly insensible to his thoughtful act of self-denial. There was in it the element of the heroic, and when was a woman ever known to be coldly indifferent to the exhibition of man's heroism?

And so the night wore on. They talked and chatted, and drew closer to the slowly dying fire; and soon there was no denying the stubborn fact that there was indeed every prospect of their spending the night in their gruesome surroundings. When this fate stared them full in the face, Miss Wilder bore the unwelcome prospect with astonishing composure. She grew quite calm, and showed, to Payson's thought, a surprising pluck. She was the first to suggest they should harbor their fuel resources, and herself extinguished the fire. Later, she submitted very acquiescingly to Payson's suggestion to rest her head on a little pillow he made for her of the dried seaweed. After a little the soft and gentle breathing that came from her lips told him that she slept.

It seemed to the man who watched over her as if some invisible power guarded her slumbers. As if Nature herself lent a helping hand, the god of the winds, or some Triton, mayhap, had with his conch bade the waves be still. For the sea lay like a sleeping lake at their feet, and some spirit of peace seemed to have entered into the air. The night grew warmer, and the wind and the waves made but a soft lullaby of sound.

A few hours later, when the dawn broke, it brought beauty and calm and cheer. All the hideousness of the night was gone. In its place was the sparkle of bright waters and the golden shimmer of the breaking sunlight. With the first rays of that rosy light Miss Wilder stirred. What Payson dreaded was her first awakening, fearing she might feel some sudden alarm. But when she opened her eyes there was no terror in them; only the beautiful bright light that comes to youth after the rest of a long sweet sleep.

"Have I really been asleep? And—oh, is it—why, it's morning!" turning a glowing face to the daylight.

"You and Aurora must have some secret sign of communication, Miss Wilder. You make your debuts at the same moment. Are you rested? Do you feel better?"

"I never felt better. I'm beginning to believe I have missed my true sphere," she gayly responded. "I should have been born a gnome. Caves seem to be my natural element. But oughtn't we to light the fire?"

"With your permission. You are keeper of the matches, you know."

In another instant the fire was lighted, and the smoke curling in great wreaths up through the opening.

"How long do you suppose it will be before—surely I hear voices. Look! Out there! Don't you see something?" cried Miss Wilder, in uncontrollable excitement, pointing to the mouth of the cave. The something proved to be some men in a boat.

Their rescuers had come at last.

A few moments later there were several heads peering down through the cleft in the rocks. And next a long rope was lowered to them.

"They're sending us a rope, but what for? You can't possibly be hauled up in that way. You'd be afraid."

"Oh no, I shan't be a bit afraid," cried the girl, to whom rescue in any shape meant a heaven-sent deliverance.

There really seemed to be no other way, and it was not many seconds before the girl was fairly seated, holding on bravely to two long ropes, securely tied and girded in by extra ones.

"I must tie you once more about the shoulders. And remember, Miss Wilder, don't look down. Keep your eyes fixed above you at the sky through the opening," was his parting injunction.

All went well till she had nearly reached the top, when, to protect herself against the jagged rocks that projected from the sides of the cleft, the girl used her hands and feet, pushing herself away from them. One particularly vigorous push loosened one of the great heavy stones. It detached itself, and the next instant was rattling down, with terrific velocity, through the great fissure.

Horror-stricken, Violet looked down. It was falling directly upon the spot where Payson was standing.

But Payson's thought, as he saw it coming, was as swift as the rock itself. Before the stone had touched the place where he stood he had flung himself into the sea. In a few seconds he had scrambled back upon the rocks again, dripping, but safe. Upon the ropes being again lowered, he was soon standing once more upon *terra firma*. His first inquiries of the men about him—men he had never seen before, fishermen apparently—was for Miss Wilder. They told him that upon the stones falling she had fainted. She was still unconscious when her uncle had carried her off in the boat, but otherwise she was unharmed.

When Payson reached his room at the hotel, two hours after, he found himself staggering about the room. His legs seemed to be parting company with his body, and his head to belong to someone else. Fatigue, hunger, and excitement had worn him out. But a light repast and a long twelve-hour sleep were all the medicine he needed. He awoke to find he had never felt in a more robust or sound condition. He could hardly wait to fling on his garments to learn how his companion had fared.

As he passed down the stairway, from the manner in which the servant-women and waiters eyed him he concluded that the story of their adventure had already become public property. He was convinced of it when, stepping out upon the piazza, ladies stopped in their promenade and their gossip to stare him out of countenance. He knew then he was a doomed man. The thing had started into its nine days' wonder of life. For himself he cared little; the battle of the tongues might wage. But he divined that Miss Wilder might not find the situation quite pleasant.

The next moment he found himself face-to-face with that young lady's uncle. Mr. Wilder greeted him with an outstretched hand and a vigorous shake of good fellowship.

"My dear fellow, I've been looking everywhere for you. We've been greatly concerned about you. You got off scot-free, hey? Not a scratch or a bruise? And you slept like a top, you say? That's fine—that's glorious. Yes, yes. Violet's coming 'round all right. A little upset, you know—cold and a bit of fever. But that'll wear off—that'll wear off. She'll be all right in a day or so. Now, my dear sir, let me make you my deepest thanks for your kindness, and for the care you took of her. She has told us everything; how you made her take your coat, and how you kept her courage up. You behaved like a man, sir, and here's my hand on it," giving Payson an elephantine grasp. He was evidently bent upon treating Payson with the tenderest consideration.

At supper, Mrs. Wilder's manner was equally cordial, if less effusive. She even linked her arm in his, later in the evening, to take a turn on the piazza with him, that she might deliver a message from Violet, a message full of kindness and friendliness. Payson divined Mrs. Wilder had noticed the questioning of those hundred inquisitive eyes, and had known how best to answer them. Payson went to bed that night in a happy dream of expectancy, the dream of seeing Violet on the morrow.

At his late breakfast he found two notes awaiting his perusal. As they bore no postmarks, he felt an ominous thrill of foreboding.

The Wilders had left; and the notes were notes of courteous, kindly, friendly farewell. Mr. Wilder explained their abrupt haste of departure by the fact of his being suddenly recalled to Boston on important business. And Miss Violet had written a line of gratitude, coupled with the assurance that she was quite herself, and perfectly well able to bear the journey. And that was all. And Payson was left with a great ache in his heart. He had counted so on seeing her again, on the friends they would grow to be, on the walks they would take, on the talks they would have. Now it was all at an end. Even the hope of seeing her again was as faint and shadowy as the making of the dream a reality.

That day and the following one seemed to Payson the longest he had ever passed. The place was becoming detestable. The truth dawned upon him that he was profoundly bored. There was nothing left to be seen, nothing to be done, except to leave, and that he should do so at once.

Awaiting the next morning the arrival of the boat, Payson strolled about the rocks. Involuntarily his steps turned toward the cliffs where he had been wont to catch his earlier glimpses of Miss Violet before he knew her. As he stood there, thinking of her, recalling just how she used to look, with her robes afloat, and her scarf floating to the breeze, like the pennant of some beautiful craft, with the rapt dream in her eyes, as if the loveliness of the scene were suffusing her in a soft rapture of content, Payson found the ache in his heart turn to a passionate thrill—a thrill that electrified every fiber of his being. Then he knew that he loved her, and that the thrill was the conscious awakening of a deep and ardent passion. He was willing now to confess to himself it had been so from the first, from the moment he had seen her. But that nascent liking had, during the long hours they had spent in the cave together, when he had had revealed to him the beautiful traits of her charming character, grown to a deeper feeling. He must see her now; he must find her, even if he went to the uttermost parts of the earth to seek her.

He would start upon the lover's pilgrimage—the pilgrimage which leads to confession.

The modern Athens has been, as a rule, more looked upon as the shrine of the Muses than as the abode of the tenderer goddess. But to Payson, Boston meant only Violet Wilder. She lived there, and the city was set about with a halo of glory.

Upon his arrival it was easy enough to discover the mundane residence of his divinity, but a much more difficult one to discover her actual whereabouts. Inquiries at a large forbidding-looking mansion fronting on the lovely Public Gardens resulted in nothing more satisfactory than the tantalizing information that the Wilders had just left Boston for Manchester, the manservant thought, but was not quite sure.

The nearest Manchester was the one down by the sea, and Payson went there by the next train. Manchester—West Manchester—was a lovely bit of shore, close to the half-moon beach of which had been built a really capital hotel. Payson found the air of the place most delicious, and the tints along the shore reminded him of the Mediterranean. But he had not come to make discoveries either in air or in tints. He had come to seek for that which he feared he should never find. His seeking her here was indeed beginning to seem a most senseless bit of folly. How could he hope, he soliloquized to himself, as he strolled later along the wide piazza of the hotel in the dawning moonlight, how could he hope—when, behold! what he hoped for stood before him. The god of love had guided his steps aright. At the farther end of the piazza a party of people were in the act of alighting from a carriage. And among them Payson's quick eye, the lover's eye, had discerned Miss Wilder. She detached herself from the party, and the next instant was coming toward him with a swift and hurried footstep. In her haste she had almost passed him by. But Payson moved toward her.

"Miss Wilder!" She started, stopped, and turned upon him an almost wildly startled glance. When she fully recognized him, she paled visibly, shaming the white roses that drooped at her belt. But she recovered herself on the instant.

"Mr. Payson, do you drop from the clouds?" holding out her hand of greeting.

"Only when I follow in the wake of a shooting star, Miss Wilder," was his gallant but somewhat agitated rejoinder.

"How good it seems to see you again! When did you come? I've been here a week. Ever since—ever since leaving Bar Harbor." She paled again. But Payson would not spare her.

"Don't you think your going away was just a trifle cruel?—without giving a fellow a chance to see you or to say good-bye? How was I to know whether you were really well or not?"

"I am sorry if you thought it rude or unkind. But"—with a slight chill in her voice—"we were obliged to go. My uncle was needed at home. Shall you be here long? I am at a friend's cottage. I must go in now. But you will come and see me, perhaps," giving him her address.

For the next week he saw her every day. But for all the progress he made, he might as well have been the other side of the moon. She seemed determined to establish spacial distances between them, yet apparently she never avoided him. On the contrary, she was not only approachable, but kind, adorably kind. She let no opportunity pass to make him the recipient of some pleasant favor. But, in spite of it all, Payson was vividly conscious he was made also the victim of a hundred subtle artifices, all of which succeeded so admirably that never by any haphazard or chance did he succeed in finding himself alone with her.

But one evening Payson's patience—the lover's patience that knows how to wait—was rewarded. Going to the cottage, on the pretense of borrowing a book, he found Miss Wilder on the veranda, looking out upon the moonlit sea. And she was alone, and there was no escape. The others had gone out to tea, she explained as she greeted him.

Perhaps it was because his chance had come, but for the first few moments Payson felt his tongue cleaving to the roof of his mouth. Perhaps it was the moonlight, and the lapping of those waves, with the memories that sound held in it for both of them.

"Miss Wilder—Miss Violet," at last Payson burst out, "tell me—tell me what it is that I have done—of what crime am I guilty?"

"Crime? Are you out of your senses, Mr. Payson?"

"No, not yet; but your manner is fast driving me out of them. Do you think it is nothing to me to know you avoid me all you can, that you put me away—"

"Oh, Mr. Payson," cried the girl, with a thrill of contrition in her voice, "I—I don't do that. I only thought—I meant—"

"And what I mean is this," said Payson, the wave of emotion so swollen it must break at last: "I mean that I have found out something since you went away from Mount Desert. I have found out that I love you as a man only can love the woman who is the one woman in the world for him. And that is what I came here to tell you."

The girl started, and stood up, stretching out her hands before her, as if to put him and his words the farther away.

"Oh, you must not—you must not say—say such things to me!"

"Why? For heaven's sake, tell me, is there any reason? You are not—" But Payson's voice broke there. He had no courage to confront the thought of her not being free.

"You must not, because," the girl went on, with a passionate, tortured ring in her tone—"because—oh, can't you see the reason? You say this because you feel you must. You think—you think people may have said—your sense of honor impels you."

"Violet, what madness are you talking? Sense of honor!" almost dazed at the joy there was in him. Then grasping the girl's hands in his trembling palm, he held them to his breast. "Listen: can a mere sense of honor make a man feel that?"

Upon the girl's upturned face Payson saw the light of his own great joy reflected.

"Ah! you believe—and, Violet, you will?"

For a moment she only looked at him, a deep, unutterable look of love, and held him still away from her as she pressed her hands against his breast. Then her answer was the droop of her beautiful head upon his shoulder.

Anna Bowman Blake (1855–1929)

Anna Bowman Blake was a New York journalist, travel writer, and the author of many books, especially on French history and politics. After her marriage to Edward William Dodd, she wrote under the name of Anna Bowman Dodd. Her most successful work was In and Out of Three Normandy Inns. *She also penned* The Republic of the Future, *a novel about New York in the year 2050, and a humorous biography of Charles Maurice de Talleyrand. She died in Paris.*

Chapter 5

Golden-Rod: An Idyl of Mount Desert

Constance C. Harrison

1880

Constance C. Harrison was among the most prolific of the Bar Harbor novelists. This is the first of three stories that she wrote about Bar Harbor in the late nineteenth century.

In Golden-Rod, *young Mr. Erskine fails to impress the "imperial ballroom belle," the widowed Mrs. Rosalie Gray, in New York City social life. Later, he hopes to find a very different playing field when he encounters her by chance in Bar Harbor one July. As Harrison notes, "better a fortnight of Mount Desert than a cycle in New York," especially when staying in the Rodick House, the "center of gaiety." The task proves as rocky for our hero as the island landscape.*

In this brief selection (which is chapter five of the novel), Harrison offers a classic description of the wonder of approaching Mount Desert Island by steamship, a standard feature in Bar Harbor novels.

On board the little steamer *Houghton* next day our party fell in with a set of Boston pilgrims, bound to the same "haven where they fain would be." Established upon deck, with shawls and books and lunch baskets, they defied the whitecaps on Penobscot Bay that frightened quite a number of their fellow passengers into seeking sofas down below. Amy, with her hands in the pockets of a long ulster (made by her brother-in-law's tailor, and the pride of her life), with a Derby hat and a cardinal silk neck-handkerchief, walked gaily up and down.

We have no coastline that will compare in beauty and variety with that of Maine. Its jagged outline breaks up into a thousand picturesque caprices of cape and bay and headland; while islands, sown like emeralds from a sieve, are scattered in countless numbers in a field of dark waves. Here masses of stern gray rock arise from the seething surf; a boat's length further on some sparkling little fiord opens through greenest meadows. Here is a cave, tinted with all the gorgeous coloring that ever dazzled Aladdin in his jeweled hall, where in the crystal depths lurk a hundred living wonders of the sea, and the great waves go booming in with a voice of thunder. Close beside it is some tiny bay, tinted like strips of the sky, fallen through from on high, and all unruffled by the wind. Under a summer sun, what voyage can be more delightful than a run in and out of the islands from Rockland to Bar Harbor? The cheery little steamer, recovering from the rude treatment of the broad Penobscot, moved soberly upon North Haven, where a rowboat was in waiting with two passengers and a trunk to be hoisted on board. After this operation they lost no time, but steamed away across the bay of Isle au Haut (pronounced "Illyhut" in the vernacular) to Deer Island, where all the population had gathered to receive an attenuated mailbag, and a few egg boxes returned from Rockland to be refilled. "And now," said the kindly captain, "you will see an island for every day in the year; and if you like to buy and settle hereabouts, we can sell you any one of them you take a fancy to, very cheap." The eldest of Thornton's boys, with a small sum of money burning holes in his trousers pockets, pursued the captain with a thousand eager questions about that last suggestion; and presently came to his father, fired with zeal for the purchase of "that nice round island over yonder; the captain says I may have it for five dollars, or this lovely little bit of a one for seventy-five cents."

In and out of the granite ledges, crowned with spruce and fir, the little steamer winds her busy way; and after passing through York Narrows, with Black Island to the northward, the first view of lovely Mount Desert Island opens before them. The beacon on Bass Harbor Head stands as her sentinel; and when they draw nearer, rounding Long Ledge, the full chain of her mountains is revealed. As the day wanes, the view changes every moment, yet never wearies. Sometimes the boat, crossing a stretch where the Atlantic swell rolls in unchecked, dances like a cork on the heaving sea; then, under the shelter of an island, the water is as calm as an inland lake. Sometimes the breeze is soft and mild as an infant's breath; then suddenly there comes a change; a glacial chill born from the bosom of a wandering iceberg descends upon them, laughed at first, but conquering in the end, and sending them on a race to the cabin for extra wraps. Contradictions and antithesis seem to be the ruling passion of Mother Nature in this region.

The first landing made at Mount Desert is Southwest Harbor, destined during the following year to be the scene of an apparition unwonted as a flamingo in a barnyard—the mysterious ship *Cambria* lying at anchor here for months, carrying under her German flag a horde of Russians awaiting the war note between their master and the Queen.

All things must have an end, the beautiful as well as others, and this fairy voyage was drawing near its close.

Leaving Southwest Harbor one has a momentary glimpse to the northward of Somes Sound, with a broad haven and splendid precipitous cliffs. Here came Henry Hudson in 1609, on his way south to explore the river now called after him. Here, a little later, the French colony of Jesuit fathers was attacked by the English pirate Argall; the station was plundered, and the godly priests murdered under the very shadow of the cross they had so triumphantly planted on the rock with chants of thanksgiving a short time before. These worthy disciples of Christ, after many days of tossing upon angry seas, in finding themselves in the glassy waters of this tranquil sound, thought it a very paradise planted in the midst of desert rocks. The cruel Englishman had expected an unresisting victim, but met a stout resistance from the plucky priests, notably from Pere Du Thet, who, when the few soldiers of the colony, panic-stricken, took to flight, fought gallantly, and found a grave upon the shore where he had hoped to make converts to the Cross. The little colony of St. Sauveur was thus rudely destroyed; but after the lapse of nearly three centuries the memory of those good men remains, and the new church recently erected at Bar Harbor is called St. Saviour, as a reminder of their devotion.

Otter Creek is passed, and many familiar spots whose very names are dear to the heart of the faithful Mount Deserter. Next the shining sands of Newport Beach, the beetling precipice of Great Head; then Frenchman's Bay, and Egg Rock with its picturesque bell tower; now the Anemone Cave, Schooner Head, the Spouting Horn, and the Porcupines, with Newport Mountain towering above all, where one may climb through woods rich in the balsam of fir and pine trees, and emerging on the summit look down nearly two thousand feet of precipice into the chafing ocean.

It is not as they had known it years ago, for the spectacle of tall hotels and "Queen Anne" cottages makes a smart modern watering place now of what was then a quaint yellow, red, and brown tinted fisher village on the coast.

In the harbor, side by side with fishing smacks and Indian canoes, are gay pleasure yachts and boats, and several times a week are emptied on its pier a horde of society seekers, alas, clad in purple and fine linen, instead of the honest band of young men and maidens, artists, students, professors, who would be boys again, who wore stout shoes, and swore to dress like tramps, and dwell like gods together through long days of glorious life in this crystal atmosphere.

The fatal tide of fashion has set that way, and having given vent to the customary Jeremiad of an aboriginal visitor to Mount Desert, it is proper to admit that there are a great many consolations left under the present state of things.

"Erskine, you had better go ashore cautiously," said the Counselor, as the little steamer touched her pier. "Ten to one there will be two rival leaders of picnic parties waiting to capture you, and bear you off in a buckboard to eat hard-boiled eggs and dismember cold chickens upon the rocks."

For once, however, this common fate was escaped, and the newcomers were only showered with cordial greetings from the picturesque groups assembled to see that great event, the arrival of the boat. Take it all in all, Bar Harbor is such an amazingly affectionate place. One grows rapturous on that wharf over friends whom one has failed to see for months, even years, in town. Snubs are forgiven, feuds are forgotten, desperate friendships are created in a breath, in this atmosphere of universal good fellowship.

It need not be said that Miss Amy North was in her element at Mount Desert. In a moment her attached family beheld her entirely submerged in the embraces of five particular girlfriends, four of whom wore brilliant Turkey red petticoats, and flourished Turkey red parasols.

Constance C. Harrison (1843–1920)

Born in Cumberland, Maryland, and raised in Richmond, Virginia, Constance Cary was a daughter of Old South aristocracy. When she married Burton Harrison, the private secretary of Jefferson

Davis, in 1867, the two moved to New York City with other "Confederate carpetbaggers," in search of new identities and financial opportunities after the defeat of the South. While her husband established a successful law practice, Mrs. Harrison became a prolific writer. In scores of articles and over thirty books of essays, short stories, plays, and novels, she waxed romantic about southern society and satirical about northern manners. Bar Harbor was a favorite summer resort for the family, and it became a locale for her stories after the Harrisons built their cottage, Sea Urchins, in the 1880s.

Chapter 6

The Summer School of Philosophy at Mt. Desert

John Ames Mitchell

1881

John Ames Mitchell's training in drawing and editing both come into play in this, his first book, which reviewers lauded as a clever and charming allegory of Bar Harbor social life. What follows are excerpts.

Various minor Summer Schools of Philosophy have lately attracted some share of public attention, it has been thought due to the great school at Mount Desert, and the interesting department of the subject to which that school is principally devoted. What follows is a humble effort at presenting some features of the methods there employed, and of the life led by the members of the school.

THE SCHOOL ASSEMBLES

Winter is departing and the island waking up.

THE PHILOSOPHY OF THE PERIPATETICS.

Canoeing is a beautiful exercise, and develops both the muscle and the heart, but is it dangerous?

We answer: No! As long as you stay in the canoe you are safe.

THE HEIGHTS OF PHILOSOPHY.

"The view at the summit of Newport Mountain this afternoon was sublime. I remained there for hours drinking it in, and now feel refreshed and elevated from such communing with nature."—From Van Twiller's epistle to his Aunt.

A SKEPTIC

who prefers Tennis to Rocking.

THE GROVES OF ACADEME.

THE PHILOSOPHY OF FAITH.
Julia's Mother (loq.):
"Julia is off sketching:—
She has a passionate
love of Art and gives
herself up to it entirely,
which saves my keeping
a constant eye upon her as
I should feel obliged to do if
she were inclined to spend her time
as frivolously as so many of
the girls one sees here."
This is
Julia.

THE STUDENTS' VIGILS.
(A sketch from memory.)

THE SUM OF ALL PHILOSOPHY.

John Ames Mitchell (1845–1918)

Born in New York City, John Ames Mitchell began his education at Phillips Exeter Academy and then enrolled at Harvard, before pursuing architectural studies in Europe. Later he settled in Boston where he worked as an architect for six years, followed by studies in painting and etching in France. When he returned to the United States he launched Life *magazine with his life's savings, persuaded that a humorous magazine could reach a sophisticated and upscale readership. While his magazine met with success, it gained greater fame when Henry Luce eventually purchased it in 1936.*

Chapter 7

A Bar Harbor Idyl

Edward A. Church

1884

This poetic rendering of the Bar Harbor flirtation underscores both its passion and ephemeral character, with a clever addition of the Harvard-Yale rivalry to the plot. (The "annex girl" in the penultimate line refers to a woman's college known as "Harvard Annex" at its founding in 1879, which became Radcliffe College in 1894.) This poem originally appeared in The Century: A Popular Quarterly, *vol. 28:4 (August 1884).*

THEY met at breakfast—she as sweet
As newly opened morning-glory;
And he a "little god" complete—
A mutual "hit!"—the old, old story!
His eager gaze, his candid stare,
Said more than Harvard lip could utter;
She read his thoughts, and, blushing rare,
Ingenuously passed the butter.

They took a pull up Frenchman's Bay,
He at the oars, she sternly steering;
Had Yale but seen his stroke that day!
Her face at each recover nearing,

A half-forbidding air it took,
    But he, the mute rebuke defying,
Cried "Pardon! but I always look
    Where I see Harvard's color flying."

They drove, of course, to Schooner Head.
    —Ah, boys are bold, but maids are mockers!—
She with Manhattan coyness said:
    "How nice you look in knickerbockers!"
He reddened, turned, she caught his eye,
    Then with the reins his fingers fumbled;
She touched his arm with half a sigh,
    And—well—in fact, he almost "tumbled."

When eve had all her burners lit,
    Down the plank walk they promenaded;
The bats across their path would flit,
    But bats that night he disregarded.
The moon o'er Ironbound shone clear;
    From boat to boat sweet notes were calling;
Yet scarce a whisper reached her ear
    Save "Let's go back; the dew is falling!"

Next morning saw them at the pier,—
    The wary youth, the pretty schemer;
Her sapphire eyes wrung out a tear
    As he, reluctant, took the steamer:
The plank is drawn, the paddles whirl,
    He turns no longer to distress her.—
Well! he secured an Annex girl,
    And she beguiled a Yale professor.

***Edward A. Church** (1844–1929)*

Edward A. Church was a Boston businessman who served as an active layman in the Church of the Disciples (Unitarian) in Boston and as longtime treasurer of the Boston Young Men's Christian Union. An amateur poet and hymn writer, Church composed "Almighty Builder" for the laying of the cornerstone of the new building of the Church of the Disciples in 1904. In the following year, he wrote "O Thou to Whom in Prayer and Praise" for the final service at the old building the church was leaving.

Chapter 8

Gypsying on Eagle Lake

Constance C. Harrison
1887

This selection is excerpted from the author's novel, Bar Harbor Days, *in which she describes the town as having gone to the dogs, literally. The recap of a summer stay of a couple of young boys, Minimus and Minor, is told by Dame Trot, a fox terrier, with assistance from her companion, Paul Pry, also a fox terrier. With remarkable grasp of the English tongue, Dame Trot describes the peculiar habit of "rocking," where couples sit aimlessly on rocks at Mount Desert: "Paul and I couldn't understand the fun of it, unless one could drop asleep. Just think of hours and hours, with no variety; only two people, and having to keep awake and talk." This selection captures the perils of overloading a buckboard and the joys of an afternoon picnic. Humans can agree with the canine assessment of Eagle Lake: "It was not hard to be happy there." "Gypsying on Eagle Lake" is the ninth chapter of* Bar Harbor Days.

"We are going to have a gypsy party at Eagle Lake, Dame Trot," said my young friend Minimus, one July morning, when I had just seen a large buckboard, drawn by four stout little mountain horses, with red tufts in their heads, swing around the circle and pull up before the front door of our house.

"Take the dogs? Why not? Of course we shall," said a man's voice on the porch, in answer to some remark from the hall inside. "They will behave splendidly; I'll answer for it."

The person who spoke was the master of the house. At his apparently unimportant and kindly observations a grin overspread the guileless countenance of Minimus. Minor, who came around from the kitchen yard, stuffing his pockets with ginger cookies, by way of incidental lunch upon the road, also smiled broadly. The children's mother, who issued from the door, her arms laden with wraps and boat cushions, parasols, and paper-covered books, wore around her lips an expression of suppressed mirth. Two of the maids, engaged in helping the buckboard man to pack in the rear of his vehicle a huge hamper of provisions, were discreetly hilarious.

Why this was, nobody told me. It may have been the reflection upon holiday faces of such a July sun as shines for Mount Desert alone. Somehow or other I could not help suspecting the entire household had been party to a plot by which Paul and I were to be admitted to the joys of gypsying on Eagle Lake. Paul, who had been inside the hall, informed me afterwards that my mistress had merely said to my master in a casual kind of way, "Of course, it'll *never* do to carry these little rascals. They are sure to be in everybody's way."

Sometimes, not often, my master would take the opposite side of a question; and this was one of those times, though of course nobody in the house had supposed such a thing to be possible!

Paul jumped several feet into the air from pure joy, and I followed his example, both of us turning a somersault upon a nasturtium bed before we got right side up again. Luckily we had no pea jackets, or fishing tackle, or anything to get before we started. We stuck there, close to the tail of the buckboard, until it left. Nobody ever found us out of the way when an expedition was ready to set off.

After a great deal of talk, and much running back into the house again for forgotten ulsters, sketchbooks, or mackintoshes, all was ready. Enough people were stopping in our house to fill the seats, with the addition of two recruits, gentlemen from, respectively, Boston and Philadelphia. The Philadelphia youth had arrived an hour beforehand in his canoe, and sat upon the rocks over the water until it was time to go. I forgot to say that a young lady from Baltimore sat there with him. I used to see such lots of that kind of aimless sitting around on rocks at Mount Desert. Paul and I couldn't understand the fun of it, unless one could drop asleep. Just think of hours and hours, with no variety; only two people, and *having* to keep awake and talk. I used to wonder what they talked about, till I found out. One time the boys and I were playing in a rock pool, behind a great, big, wide open, red umbrella. The umbrella did not know we were there, and we couldn't see a thing for the umbrella. But we *heard*! Just get Minimus and Minor to tell you what we heard. I thought our fellows would die of trying to keep in their giggles.

The Boston gentleman invited to join our party arrived at the house on a bicycle. When he saw the canoe young man was already there, he did not look particularly gay. I wonder why? I suppose it was a race. When our boys race, the one who gets in last is always pretty grumpy for a while. However, it soon came to be the Philadelphian's turn to lose his spirits—when he was put on the buckboard seat beside my mistress's maiden aunt from Kalamazoo, who asked him a good many questions about botany and geology. On the seat immediately behind the driver sat the bicycle young man. Next him a large, round, red straw hat, with a steeple-crown and lots of red feathers. When the hat turned around you saw it had a very pretty girl inside; but from the rear it was principally hat. Next to the red hat, Minimus was perched. He had a rubber sling, and from his pocket took out no end of buckshot, which rattled through the trees along the roadside during the whole course of our drive.

"Look there! Did you see that?" Minimus would cry, hailing Minor, sitting next his mother in the rear. "I don't believe I ever came nearer hitting a chipmunk in my life." Which was indisputable.

Up hill and down dale the buckboard rolled merrily. When we reached places where the road went sharply down into a valley, to mount immediately a steep ascent, the driver gave a soft little chirrup and off the four horses dashed at a gallop, never pausing till they reached the first "thank-ye-marm" on the hill beyond. The first time this occurred, my mistress's maiden aunt became panic-stricken. She seized the coat sleeve of the canoe young man. She wore black kid gloves, too long in the fingers, and I think she must have pinched him. What else could account for the frown upon his brows, and a certain smothered exclamation heard by me alone?

At Eagle Lake there is a sort of wayside inn, in a clearing among the pines near the steamboat wharf. We went in to inquire about the boats we had engaged by telephone. The young man who informed us it was all right, and preceded us to the spot of embarkation, wore a glistening silver shield upon the lapel of his coat. Minor's quick eyes discerned the legend inscribed thereon. Falling behind, he called the attention of his brother to the fact that their guide was a "champion contortionist," having won his badge by distinction in the field of this especial branch of athletic accomplishment.

"When we come back this way, if there's time, he says maybe he'll contort for us," added Minor.

"Well, I don't *mind* seeing him," said the world-weary Minimus. "But we've been to all the India rubber men that Barnum could scare up!"

Three rowboats, courtesying on the rippled surface of a jewel-bright lake, received our numbers. Minor, on whom his mother was fond of depending for her aquatic pleasures, claimed one pair of the oars in her boat. I sat in my mistress's lap, watching the strong, regular stroke of our youthful sculler. With his Tam o'Shanter set on the back of his brown head, the loose collar of his blue flannel shirt unbuttoned, the familiar frown upon his brow, with flushed cheeks and arms bared for action, he was a picture of health and happiness. In the bow sat the bicycle young man, who seemed to have a great deal to say to my mistress, with very little variety in the theme, which was the perfections of Baltimore girls in general, and of a certain young lady in a red straw hat, in particular. My mistress listened in a patient sort of way. She seemed to find pleasure enough in looking before her at the green hillsides curving down to form the hollow which holds this inland sea. I noticed that from shore to shore of the two extremities of the lake she said about five words. And yet the bicycle young man told the canoe young man, in my hearing, while they were having their cigarettes after luncheon, a little later, that he had never found my mistress so agreeable before.

In mid-lake there passed us the toy steamboat *Wauginett*, with her quota of tourists, bound for the ascent of Green Mountain. Looking up the seared and barren mountainside we saw a train creeping cautiously down the perilously steep incline. Minor said it was a serpent who had his lair in the mountaintop, descending to gorge himself with mortals. Willing victims they are, apparently, since all summer long the little railway does a thriving business. Tourists in high hats, with paper collars and—odious word!—gripsacks; tourists in

Derby hats, with baggy English trousers; tourists in rainbow flannel coats, with heelless canvas shoes—come and go, with appropriately attired females in their wake.

Everybody should see Green Mountain from the top, they say, and almost everybody does. Way up on its denuded summit is a great hotel, which, when the electric lights are set ablaze at nightfall, looks from below like an illuminated lyre.

Eagle Lake has another most important mission to fulfill beside that of carrying pleasure-seekers upon her billowy bosom. From her crystalline depths flows the great water supply of Bar Harbor. Silvery brook trout, of noble proportions, are caught in this favored lake, and in winter fishermen from the village take them in numbers through holes cut in the ice.

After a couple of miles or more of steady rowing we had reached the trysting place. One interesting feature of our boat was that it carried the luncheon hamper, and myself. So when we got there first, driving our bows in between a huge boulder and a smooth, wide stone, I naturally felt that the success of the occasion was established.

We scrambled ashore, finding our way around the sandy beach to a spot delightfully overshadowed by birches and fragrant balsams. Scattered about were gray masses of granite, overgrown with rock fern. On the edge of the woods behind us grew gnarled and twisted cedars, forming natural armchairs. Waves that were hardly more than wrinkles on the blue made a gentle motion amid the sedge grass at our feet. From the forest depths came a smell of ferns and balm and spicery. It was not hard to be happy there.

By the time the other boats came leisurely ashore, Minor and the bicycle young man had worked wonders in the way of preparation. Driftwood, distorted roots made gray and polished by the action of waves and sunshine, broken boughs of fir and cedar, dried bracken and pinecones were heaped together against a rock and set ablaze. A tablecloth laid on the dry sand was decked around the edge with ferns and buttercups. Then Minor and the bicycle young man unpacked the basket. Goodness! How my mouth watered. It is painful to have to confess it, in a literary fox terrier of aesthetic taste, but when I saw the things that came out of that hamper I had to yelp!

Paul heard me from his boat and yelped back. He told me, when he reached my side, that the air of the lake had made him positively ravenous. He did not think it possible to hold out two minutes longer. For my dear Paul's sake I then was guilty, for the first time in my life, of a most unladylike action. I walked right down to the middle of the tablecloth, between the mayonnaise salmon and the deviled lobster, and helped myself to a chicken wing. Strangely enough, nobody but my mistress saw me do it, and she looked so distressed by my breach of good manners that my heart smote me. Although I had carried that wing some distance off, I took it back to her and laid it in her lap. Then I rolled over on my back and cringed, a way we fox terriers have of asking to be pardoned.

"No, thank you, Trotty," said my mistress, laughing. "You may have it now, you naughty little girl."

By the time Paul and I had crunched that bone between us, and had returned to join the company, there was the canoe young man, with a dishtowel pinned around his waist, and a chef's cap made of a newspaper, cooking beefsteaks on the embers of our fire. There was the young lady with the red straw hat, cutting up tomatoes on a bed of ice. There was the maiden aunt, without her black kid gloves, making coffee. There was the master of our house, lying on a sand bank in the sun, under the impression he was doing the main part of everybody's work. There was Minimus, barelegged, in the shallow water, catching minnows in a pail. There were the bicycle young man, cooling champagne in the lake, and Minor cracking ice for it.

A newly married couple I haven't mentioned before, chiefly because of their temporary objection to be included with unemotional humanity, had retired to a little distance and were heaping up sandhills to cover with their rugs. They seemed to think the shore of Eagle Lake was a desert of the most approved pattern—the place people, just before and after their honeymoon, talk about flying to, in company with the chosen of their hearts. Lastly, there was our mistress calling upon everybody to come and eat her feast.

Oh, that feast! For the only time that I can remember such a thing, Paul and I got more than we cared to eat. No stingy, jaw-breaking dog biscuit, no chopped things from other people's plates. It was grand! Glorious!

As for Minor and Minimus, those two boys began at A and ate down to Z, on the bill-of-fare. Minor broke down first, and put away his plate with a sigh of genuine regret. But that astonishing Minimus kept it up some time longer. For a boy of slender build, with rather a sentimental cast of face, he is the most valiant trencherman of my acquaintance.

We lounged and dozed and chatted quietly during an hour or so of that golden afternoon. Then, consigning our traps to a boatman, who, towing two of the boats, rowed in the third, on his return to our starting point, we set out to cross on foot the carry between the lake and Jordan's Pond.

"Say, rather, to plunge headlong into Fairy Land," cried the romantic young lady of our party.

If Fairy Land be green, and still, and dewy; a solitude of garnered fragrance, of fir boughs shutting out the blue above; of fern, knee high to mortals, a very jungle for fairy feet to err in; of moss under foot, moss coating the rocks scattered along the narrow trail, moss on tree trunks, moss everywhere; of hidden brooks and birds, that made music for the wayfarer; of clustering crow's foot, arbutus, shepherd's pipe, and partridge berry—then was our lady right.

We met two young men in knickerbockers carrying canoes upon their heads. They looked like some queer kind of perambulating turtles, as they bobbed up and down the rough path, and from under their birch-bark roofs came the smothered strain of—

"The flowers that bloom in the spring, tra-la."

"Oh!—" broke out impatiently the master of our house.

"Bother the flowers of spring!" chimed in Minor and Minimus, interrupting him.

"That was not what I intended to say," remarked the master, mildly; "it's not half strong enough to express my feelings. I might as well be back in New York, with the hand organs."

"Will this please you better?" said the bicycle young gentleman, who, among other accomplishments, had a very sweet voice, in singing:

"Under the greenwood tree,
Who loves to lie with me,
And turn his merry note
Unto the sweet bird's throat.
Come hither, come hither, come hither,
Here shall he see
No enemy
But winter and rough weather."

"More, more, I prithee more," said everybody; and then the woods rang with songs and glees and catches. They sang all they knew, from "Scotland's Burning," and "Three Blind Mice," to that robust old English hunting chorus:

"A southerly wind, and a cloudy sky,
Proclaim it a hunting morning,
Before the sun rises away we will fly,
Dull sleep and a downy bed scorning.
To horse, my brave boys, and away,
Bright Phoebus the hills is adorning;
The face of all nature looks gay,
'Tis a beautiful scent-laying morning.
Hark—hark, forward,
Tirrila, tirrila, tirrila!"

As the last joyous *tirrila* died in the silence of the wood we saw daylight at the end of a bowery vista. Paul and I bounded ahead, the lads upon our heels. We came out upon the pebbly beach of another perfect lake, locked in the chill embrace of cliffs that rose on either side. Here more boats awaited us, and we again embarked, to dawdle away the remainder of the day.

Halfway across the lake, the boat with Minor in it came to a standstill, then veered off under the shadow of the cliff. Well did I know what he had in mind, and greatly did I lament my ill fortune in being in the other boat. I saw the fly rod unpacked, and the landing net bestowed upon the boatman. Then Minor stood up and cast, while the hearts of Minimus and Paul and I swelled with honest pride in reflecting upon our connection with the hero of the hour.

For we knew he would have luck. None of us were at all surprised when one of our gentlemen remarked, "Hullo! That boy has got a rise." All other business was suspended, while we watched him tire his prey. Presently, down went the landing net, and up came a splendid lake trout. Then only, an exultant cry arose from Minimus.

"I couldn't help that squeal," said the little boy, repentantly. "It was just squeezed out of me."

It was not till towards sunset that the fishing boat came up with ours. Minor's first prize, weighing a pound and a half, had been followed by several smaller. His face, burned to a uniform deep red, expressed purest satisfaction.

Why, ah, why did that summer's sun go slanting to its rest—one half the lake in shadow, the rest like molten silver? Did it not serve to remind the master of our house that a buckboard was awaiting us on shore?

I don't know, however, but that one of the pleasantest features of a buckboard party is the drive home in the cool of evening, amid the uprising thyme-y fragrance of the fields, the spicy odors of the forest, and the waft of brine that comes into one's nostrils when a turn of the road brings to view a glimpse of tossing sea.

As we drove through the village, we saw signs at some of the hotels that those inevitable "hops" were beginning to be in progress. I hope I am not a misanthrope, but I must protest against the extraordinary fancy for this form of entertainment. Why sensible people, who journey here to rid themselves of the wear and chafe of work-a-day employment, or society monotony, should consider it a joy to put on evening clothes and caper in those melancholy halls, I know not! I heard a gentleman say once that such entertainments bear to those of the actual world of fashion the relation of cleaned gloves to new ones. But the ladies cried him down, and told him his comment was neither just nor witty. And they went on as before. They generally do.

It is true that men in flannel shirts and knickerbockers are no longer to be seen waltzing with girls in low-cut gowns that have served their seasons in the ballrooms of Delmonico and in Washington. The men who do not care to dress now haunt the verandas and discuss the crowd inside. And ah! How pretty those girls inside are, to be sure, after their days spent rowing, canoeing, climbing, riding in Bar Harbor air. From all quarters of the continent they gather, and unite in a veritable rosebud garland! Yes, one forgives the hotel hops for bringing them together!

***Constance C. Harrison** (1843–1920)*

Born in Cumberland, Maryland, and raised in Richmond, Virginia, Constance Cary was a daughter of Old South aristocracy. When she married Burton Harrison, the private secretary of Jefferson Davis, in 1867, the two moved to New York City with other "Confederate carpetbaggers," in search of new identities and financial opportunities after the defeat of the South. While her husband established a successful law practice, Mrs. Harrison became a prolific writer. In scores of articles and over thirty books of essays, short stories, plays, and novels, she waxed romantic about southern society and satirical about northern manners. Bar Harbor was a favorite summer resort for the family, and it became a locale for her stories after the Harrisons built their cottage, Sea Urchins, in the 1880s.

Chapter 9

The Colonel's Last Campaign

Ervin Wardman

1892

Retired from a career of fighting Indians along the western frontier, Colonel Hardeservice travels to Bar Harbor with his family to engage in his "last campaign," which is to marry off his two daughters. His brilliant strategy secures two fine suitors, though in love as well as in battle, things don't always go exactly as planned.

"The Colonel's Last Campaign" was originally published in The Century: A Popular Quarterly*, 44 (August 1892): 508–17.*

"I suppose," said Major Hardeservice one day to his wife, when their daughter Eleanor, seven years old, was looking into a mirror and tossing her bright curls vainly, "that Nellie will marry a rich man."

"Oh, yes, indeed," said little Mrs. Hardeservice with a touch of pride. "Nellie will be very handsome, like you, Frank—straight and tall and fair."

Major Hardeservice had been straight and fair, and he was still handsome, with a firm and almost dashing carriage; but several years of service on the frontier under a burning sun, where in summer the hot air, from whatever direction it blew, came over a dazzling white plain, had turned a fair complexion to a permanent red. The Major's uniform, too, measured several inches more around the belt than when, as a slender lieutenant, he had assisted Miss Elizabeth Marwin to change her name. No doubt if a blush could have vied with his high color, his wife would have seen that the Major was pleased, for he was proud of his good looks, and Eleanor might have inherited her father's vanity.

"But Bess," said the big soldier, pulling a little dark-eyed creature up to his broad knee, and pressing a heavy mustache against the soft cheek, "will marry for love, dear. And she will make a good wife for a fortune-less soldier like me. She is like her mother."

The hot winds of the desert, and the blinding glitter of snow on crusted fields, had not spoiled the delicacy of Mrs. Hardeservice's cheek, and her blush was evident enough. It was such a pretty blush that the Major heightened it with his lips, and then went stalking out so heavily that the weight of his boots on the boardwalk could be heard until he reached the parade ground.

In this way it came about that the family always thought and spoke of Eleanor as the future wife of some man whose fortune could be measured only by the beauty of his wife. That such a man would be worthy there never was any doubt.

But this was almost twenty years before the summer when Colonel and Mrs. Hardeservice and the Misses Hardeservice were spending the summer at Bar Harbor.

The pretty Eleanor, when she was fifteen years old (she did not deny three months later that she was sixteen), had been sent East to her Aunt Helen to receive in New York the social education befitting a rich man's wife. At that time she was as vain and as coquettish as any young girl who is pretty and fully aware of her beauty.

When little Bess, out on the withered stretches of Colorado, read her sister's letters about New York, she thought Eleanor a very fine lady, for Bess's big eyes had seen as yet only forts, and soldiers, and army officers who petted her, and big, square houses as hideous as dull red paint could make them.

On the night when Miss Eleanor was "to come out," there was an additional military erectness to the Major's figure over two thousand miles away from New York. Mrs. Hardeservice was in as much of a flutter as if she herself were that night to make a pretty courtesy to full-fledged society. Bess, now fourteen, was in an ecstatic dream in which magnificent gowns, and wonderful music, and oppressively fragrant flowers set her head in a wild whirl. The sentry who paced out the dark night near the Major's quarters wondered at the lateness of the hour when the last light in the officer's house went out.

After this came long letters of afternoon teas, receptions, dinner parties, cotillions, and countless other entertainments, so that Bess lay awake at night and pictured dukes and royal princes kneeling before Nell, while glittering palaces and fairy gardens danced before her eyes. She was a little disappointed when she received a photograph on the back of which was written, "To my dearest Bess, from her sister in her coming-out gown." Bess had expected to see a crown on the grand lady's head, whereas she was dressed very simply in white. But she was a very beautiful woman, and Mrs. Hardeservice looked at the picture many times that day.

Bess had gone to bed when Mrs. Hardeservice, looking at the Major as she spoke to him of Eleanor, saw that he was dozing. His hand was clenched around a newspaper so that the edges had split. She went up to him with tears in her eyes, and threw her arms around his neck.

"Frank," she said, half sobbing, "I want her."

The Major sprang to his feet. His arm shot out, his finger pointing steadily.

"I can march it in thirteen hours!" he cried, and then rubbed his eyes. "Nell, dear," he added with a short laugh, as if he were ashamed, "I have been fighting Indians again." He looked regretful to find himself in post instead of in the field. She was crying softly to herself when she went upstairs.

Eleanor was twenty, and her father was a colonel, when his horse, carrying him over the plain at a hard gallop, plunged a leg into a prairie dog hole. The heavy Colonel was carried home white and limp, and Caesar, the horse, was shot to end his suffering. The Colonel lay in bed for three months, and then went on the retired list. The family moved East, and after living in New York for a few months found a quiet little home in Mount Vernon, where the Colonel read the military publications, and army and navy notes in the newspapers—and fretted.

As for Eleanor, she had grown into a wonderfully beautiful woman, and her triumphs were many. She was then tall and slender, with shoulders which marked her spirit and pride. She held them up and back, and when she shrugged them it was like the gesture of a woman who ruled a people. Her throat and neck were marvelously beautiful. They were soft, and yet there was strength in them. Her head was firmly poised, and the hues of her hair were radiant. When she was pleased her eyes, and lips, and every curve of her features, smiled. When she was indifferent her face was like white marble.

Her winters were spent in New York with her aunt, and though no one doubted that she was, as the newspapers spoke of her, a reigning belle, she did not get married. Not that she had no opportunities. There were hints without end in the publications that balance the accounts of society's ledgers. The smart young men who dawdled on the outer circles of her admirers could tell who was going to marry her. Sometimes they let slip the secret; sometimes they declared that they could not betray honorable confidences. There were mothers of daughters who frowned when desirable men followed in the haughty Miss Hardeservice's train. There were mothers of light-headed young men, possessed of ample fortunes, who trembled at the same time. And yet Miss Hardeservice did not get married. There was only one family that did not wonder at this. The Colonel was a little worried, for he was poor, but his serenity of mind never deserted him about his elder daughter's judgment. Mrs. Hardeservice was content to have her daughter, if only during the summers, and Bess loyally scoffed at every man who offered his name and fortune to her sister. Bess saw a little of Eleanor's world. She stayed in it for one winter. She was not abashed, but after that she chose to remain at home, and while her sister danced gaily or impassively in the social whirl, got her name in the society columns daily, and gracefully repulsed young men who swore that they would shoot themselves if she did not marry them, Bess read the *Army and Navy Journal* to her soldier father while he indulged in stolen naps, unmindful of social strife or Indian wars.

When Miss Hardeservice confessed to the Colonel one day, as her fingers played with his gray locks, that she was weary of it all, and begged him to take her to Bar Harbor on a family trip, where they could amuse one another, the Colonel, as he always did to every proposal of hers, cheerfully consented. He went to his desk, looked at his slender surplus in the bank, wrinkled his brows a little, and made one more plunge into his account.

It was at Bar Harbor that Colonel Hardeservice began and brilliantly closed his last campaign. While the family adhered strictly to their plan of enjoying themselves very quietly and simply, it was not surprising that Eleanor should find at Bar Harbor friends who were unwilling to allow her to keep in the social background. But when it was proved after argument, pleadings, and protestations that she was determined in her resolve, her ardent friends did not force their admiration to the point of driving themselves into sympathetic retirement. Her father, valiant soldier that he was, stood before Eleanor. Her friends began to know him. They had not seen his like before. His candor, his freshness, his freedom from conventional restraint, and his fine, open self-reliance, nourished and ripened on frontier posts, caught the spirits of all who met him. It was then that the Colonel became a lion. He danced, he told stories of Western life, he promenaded the long verandas, debutantes leaning on his arm. Colonel Hardeservice was the central figure of Bar Harbor, and in defending his daughter from her admirers and suitors he gave back to society not only Miss Hardeservice, but her father.

The Colonel saw at first glance wherein Eleanor had been at fault. It was not true that there were no men who were her equals. There were many—too many. Only an old campaigner could pick from the flower of this army the most gallant and worthy captain. So while the Colonel conducted armies of young pedestrians up Newport Mountain, led dashing cavalry troops in buckboards over the island of Mount Desert, and watched social maneuvers with a critical eye, he searched carefully for his chief aide. In the flush of his victories he went beyond military operations. He planned a naval invasion of the dark-hued island which lay before his hotel. Seated in a fickle canoe managed by a young woman whose color was as fresh as the sea air—the Colonel had never touched an oar or a paddle in his life—he saw his fleet ground on the shore of the invaded land, and, standing up in his treacherous craft, gaily waved his straw hat and proclaimed the island a province of Mount Desert.

Those were joyous days for the Colonel. The eyes of the fashionable world were upon him. But he did not allow himself to forget his duty to Eleanor. His keen eye was always on the alert. The man whom he sought he soon found. At the same time he made a discovery which caused him, a father whose whole thoughts were devoted to the interest of his daughter, no little mental turmoil.

There were two men toward whom the Colonel's attention was drawn. He liked them both, and their admiration for him was shown in many ways. They were both wholly unlike the Colonel and wholly unlike each other. What made it hard for the Colonel to do his duty was that his heart went out at the very start to the younger of the two men. And he was poor. He liked Alfred Strong because Strong reminded him of the army. He was bold, vigorous, impetuous, and a little intolerant. He spoke rapidly in an argument, almost nervously, but he talked well, for in his life as a newspaperman, from reporter to editor, he had seen a good deal of the world—"A good deal," he himself said, "which a man would be better for not seeing and knowing."

Philip Malcolm, Strong's friend, on the other hand, had never earned a penny in his life. He had been constantly in Miss Hardeservice's court for three years. He was rich, he was slow, and he was grave. The Colonel had great respect for his good sense. He decided that Malcolm was a most desirable son-in-law, and although he would have preferred Strong, he accepted the conditions, soldier-like, and was firm in his duty.

The striking difference between the two friends, Strong and Malcolm, was something like this:

"You are a lucky dog, Phil, to have your disposition," said Strong once, when Malcolm came up to the editorial rooms after a rambling trip abroad. "If I had your money, it would kill me. I should be chasing fancies from the North to the South Pole. I couldn't keep still, should get out of breath and run myself to death—die from heart failure."

"I work just as hard in my way," Malcolm answered, "as you do. I am forced to amuse myself. That is the hardest work in the world. I'm not fit for real, honest work. You can make your own living. That ought to be satisfaction enough."

He turned his dark eyes to look after something that was beyond his reach.

"Paint! Paint!" cried Strong. "You paint well. That last bit of yours was good. Everyone says so. How long did it take you? Two years!" exclaimed the editor. "I should drive at a picture night and day, spoil it in no time, and smash the canvas on a chair. You have patience; paint and do something."

Malcolm smiled at his ardor. "My dear fellow," he said, "it is easy enough for you to say that. That feeling is part of you. But I am different, and I make the best of it." Nevertheless, he looked discontented.

What made the Colonel attached to Strong was the editor's iconoclastic way of smashing at things.

"A newspaper man," said Strong to him, "is a freak of nature. He is shut out from those things which most people regard as the best part of life. He should never get married, for instance. It isn't fair to his family. He is an independent slave—a slave so long as he earns his living; independent when he starves. His whole self is put away, checked at the door, you might say, when he goes to his editorial desk. He gets no rest and no consideration, because every one around him lives at the same high tension, until he breaks down. Then there is a flurry. Everyone is shocked. His paper sends him to Europe—can't do enough for him; but his nerves are gone. They are on so fine an edge that inactivity jars them. Look at me—thirty-five, a young man, and my paper has to exile me to Bar Harbor for the summer. I should not have lasted here a week," he added with a smile, "if you had not come along to cheer me up. It's frightfully dull and flat. When I was a reporter I could work thirty-six hours at a stretch without a wink of sleep or a bite to eat save a sandwich wherever I could grab it. I would then go home, sleep ten hours, eat a good breakfast, and report at the office, bright and smiling for another fast. Now—why, it would kill me now," he said with a laugh.

"A soldier, too," said the Colonel. "Just like us. But you wouldn't change it."

Strong leaned back in his chair and smiled into the keen old eyes of the soldier.

"No, I wouldn't," he said, "not for the world. I live on it. The excitement and stimulus of it would keep me alive."

"So it does; so it did with me," cried the Colonel, warmly. He wished that Strong were wealthy. "I would give—oh, it's all over with me now," he added gloomily.

After this talk Strong held first place in the Colonel's estimation.

Strong was on the veranda of the Colonel's hotel, talking with the veteran and Malcolm, when he first met Miss Hardeservice. She came walking up slowly from the water, a jacket trailing in her hand. There were then two small spots of color in her cheeks, which looked brighter than they were above the white of her yachting gown. It was after dinner, and the slanting sun sent shining flashes through her hair. When she sat down with them to rest, her several winters in New York showed in her face, for it became pale; but at times, as she talked, a touch of pink was in her cheek again.

"That color will refuse to come in two years more," said Strong to himself. He looked at her while he chatted with the little dark-eyed one, as he called the younger Miss Hardeservice.

"She is older than she looks," he thought. "Twenty-eight, or twenty-nine; no, twenty-eight." He wronged her by two years. After a while he drifted into conversation with her alone. It was perfectly aimless. He became a trifle impatient with her. "She poses," he said mentally.

When he and Malcolm were walking to their hotel, he broke out suddenly, "She is handsome."

"Who is handsome?" said Malcolm.

"Why, Miss Hardeservice, of course." He knew all about Malcolm's suit, but he was very frank with his friend.

"I didn't like her mannerisms," Strong went on; "that is, I thought she assumed a weariness of some things. Perhaps she piqued my vanity by appearing to be a little bored. Isn't she just a bit of a coquette?" he blurted out.

"N—no, she isn't," answered Malcolm. "I once thought she was." He stopped for a minute. "But she is perfectly frank with men. I do not know of a single case where she has not been sincere."

"Well, I like the little one better," said Strong. "She is full of good sense, and she knows a deal. She rests me. She's calm and placid, like the water down there. Her sister is more like those straight trees up on the hill."

Malcolm gave him no answer.

"But I must say, Phil," Strong went on, "that I have never seen a more handsome woman. She carries herself superbly. She seems to be all that a man could picture to himself. If she would only feel! Do you know," he said earnestly, "I can't get it out of my head that she poses. Hang it, Phil!" he jerked out in his quick way, forgetting his friend, "I think that girl wants to marry money."

"I don't believe it," answered the other, quietly, looking up over the hill. "No; you will like her better. She is much like her father."

"He is a sterling old soldier and a fine gentleman," said Strong. "I like him. I like the little one. I think I like them all, but I like the Colonel best."

It did not take the Colonel long, with his fine perceptions, to discover that Strong was falling in love with his younger daughter. This complicated affairs, but it eased his mind, for he would have found it against his inclination to oppose the editor had he tried to win Eleanor. Now he had only to broaden his field of operations and to make use of his military talents in massing his forces or performing flank movements. So the Colonel's ruddy face beamed, and his heart was light; but this campaign was no easy one.

"My troops," he used to say when holding councils of war with himself, "are undisciplined. They have a tendency to lose their heads." And this was quite true, though perhaps not in the sense which the Colonel meant it. They rather bewildered him at times. The forces were often thrown into utter confusion, so that he could not direct them all.

One of the difficulties was that Strong was impartial in his attentions. He was as uncertain as the wind. Malcolm's suit made little headway. It was impossible to tell whether he felt shy or hopeless.

There was also one phase of the situation which the commander-in-chief failed to take in: Strong and Malcolm were not so cordial to each other as they had been. This was scarcely the fault of Strong. He believed in a fair fight and the laurels to the victor. Malcolm, on the other hand, could not take up arms against a friend. He was never sure of his own position, and was even in more doubt about Strong. He was a shuttlecock on a battledore held by an irresponsible hand. If he went canoeing with Bess, it was because Miss Hardeservice and Strong were on the water together. If he found himself playing tennis with Miss Hardeservice for a partner, it was because Bess and Strong had already formed an alliance. Realizing this, Malcolm felt uncomfortable. But the Colonel was untiring in the use of his tactics, so that in the end he usually had the supreme satisfaction of seeing the battle wage as he wished. Then he would draw aloof and survey the field with a calm dignity and a soldier's pride. One could almost fancy him sweeping a plain with his field glass. As he examined the war maps in his brain, his smile grew more eloquent and his face more ruddy.

One night, when he gave Bess a good-night kiss, he pinched her cheek affectionately, and looked down into her dark eyes with such a meaning glance that his daughter blushed furiously and ran away from him, involuntarily trying to hide her treacherous cheeks with her hands.

"Strong is in love with our Bess, dear," he said to his wife.

"I think he is, Frank," answered his wife, complacently.

"This has been known to me for sometime," said the Colonel, nodding his gray head sagely.

"I don't think that Bess is very—fond of him," she answered, hesitating over the word.

"Don't you?" said he, with a mysterious smile. "He is just the husband for Bess, frank, brave, able, and—handsome," he added, looking at himself in a glass. "You aren't opposed to it, are you?" he asked anxiously.

"Not in the least. Bess will marry the man she loves. She could not be made to do otherwise. She has a great deal of spirit, only she seldom shows it."

"But she likes Strong."

"Yes, she does; but Bess is very shy. If she loved a man, she would be more likely to retreat from him. I should say that she was more likely to love Mr.—a man like—well, a man like Malcolm."

"You don't mean to say," cried the Colonel, jumping up in alarm, "that—"

"Oh, dear, no," cried little Mrs. Hardeservice, frightened by her husband's voice.

"What do you mean, then?" he asked in a relieved tone.

"I think that Mr. Strong is in love with Bess, that Mr. Malcolm has always been in love with Nell, but that such an idea never entered Bess's little head, while Nell doesn't care for either of them. Nell seems to be tired of everyone but us. She says that she is going to spend the winter at home. She has written to her aunt, and Helen is greatly vexed about it."

"My dear," said the Colonel, smoothing his ruffled dignity, "you should see with my eyes. Nell will be engaged to Malcolm before we leave this place."

"Never mind, Frank," answered his wife, gently; "it will all come out right."

"How blind women are!" reflected the son of Mars; and he smiled serenely.

Perhaps Strong and Malcolm first confessed to themselves that their relations were a little strained on the evening when they just escaped a serious accident. They were out canoeing with the two sisters. Strong managed a canoe with fine skill. His boat was a mere shell, and his quick arms drove it through the still water like a knife blade. It was as delicately poised as a spinning bicycle wheel, and Strong, with another person in the craft, could keep it at all times on a perfect balance. He and the younger Miss Hardeservice were shooting about on the water before the island, while Malcolm and Miss Hardeservice, in a much heavier boat, were following in their wake. Strong wheeled his frail craft around in a pretty half-circle, a streak of white behind them showing their course. Then with a long sweep of his arm, showing brown and sinewy where his sleeves were up-rolled, he sent the canoe skimming over the water, and drew in his paddle. This circular course brought them nearer Malcolm and Miss Hardeservice. Strong and the younger sister watched the water drip from the shining paddle as they drifted.

Malcolm was propelling his heavy canoe vigorously, and his boat promised to cross Strong's bow. He seemed a little excited.

Miss Hardeservice's back was toward them, and she held her glove up where the sun touched her cheek.

They were not twenty yards away, and would cross very near the light canoe, when suddenly Malcolm's paddle stopped as he leaned forward saying something earnestly; his boat swerved, and came straight toward the other canoe. Strong's paddle was lying across his lap.

"Look out, Phil!" he shouted, as he seized it, and thrust it into the water; "you will cut us down!" His paddle gleamed behind him, and the canoe sprang ahead. Malcolm had not seen them. Before he could lift his hand, his boat shot along the stern of Strong's, grazing it and sending a shiver over the lighter craft.

"Sit still, sit still," said Strong in a low voice to the younger Miss Hardeservice, as the canoe tipped and rocked. Her face was pale. He brought his boat around until he was close up to Malcolm. He looked at his friend, and then at Miss Hardeservice. Malcolm was dazed, but she had a fine light on her beautiful face. Strong's eyes flashed, and when he spoke his voice was trembling.

"You just missed drowning us all, Phil," he said curtly, and turned his canoe toward the shore. His glance fell on his companion as his paddle flashed back and forth.

"I hope you were not frightened," he said, trying to smile.

"Oh, no," she answered; "you were so quick that I had no time to know that there was any danger." But her lip quivered.

Strong did not seem to hear her. His lips were pressed together, and where his straight rows approached each other there was a little knot.

Malcolm apologized to him that evening.

"I nearly made a fatal blunder," he said, "and I am ashamed enough of myself. You saved us all, Fred. Thank you very much," and he tried to wring the other's hand. "I was thrown out of my senses," he went on, hesitating. "I—I was greatly surprised by something. Don't be so stiff about it, Fred," he added, with a rising color. "Miss Hardeservice—that is, I made a terrible blunder."

"All's well that ends well," answered the other, with a little laugh that was slightly harsh.

Not until the season was nearing its end did Colonel Hardeservice lose faith in his strategy, and not even then would he believe that he had been entirely mistaken in his plan of conducting his campaign. But he was harassed by misgivings. Apparently he had won the day. Strong was nearly always with Bess, and Miss Hardeservice was more kind to Malcolm than she had ever been before; but there was now an open restraint between everyone. Strong and Malcolm had no more to do with each other than courtesy and civility demanded. The Colonel himself did not find the editor so entertaining or frank as he had been. Eleanor was the most natural of them all. She was as dignified as always, and if she were more bored than usual, she did not allow herself to show it. Mrs. Hardeservice thought Bess was growing pale, and hinted at malaria. The Colonel pooh-poohed at her alarm, but went off for a drive with his favorite child.

"Your old father is unhappy, Bess," he said, as they followed the winding road down by the sea. "What is the matter with us, anyway?" He cut his horses sharply.

She looked at him with startled eyes.

"I think we are all homesick, Papa," she answered softly. She was looking away from his eyes. "It is too gay for us here," she continued, laughing. "Look at that." A merry party in a large buckboard passed them on the road, sending up a cloud of white dust. Bright ribbons fluttered and colored caps danced as the party greeted the popular Colonel and his daughter.

"You are an old soldier, and I am nothing but a soldier's daughter, and I think we are—we are out of our element."

The Colonel scented danger afar, but he could not locate it. He looked down at his daughter. Her dark eyelashes were low, but he thought he saw something bright there. He put out his big hand over her little one, trying to stroke it in a clumsy way.

"Would you like to go home?" he asked.

She turned her soft eyes to his. They were wet.

"Yes—thank you, Papa," she said. Her words were only breathed. She hid her face on his sleeve for a moment, and the grizzled warrior slashed his horses furiously as if with a saber.

The Hardeservices were going to leave Bar Harbor. Everyone was sorry. The last season's debutantes begged the Colonel to stay until they went. He smiled at them all, and, shaking his gray head, reminded them that he was a soldier. Strong did not come near them for two days. Malcolm was unchanged. They were to start on Saturday. On Friday, Strong, reaching the top of Newport after a rapid climb, found Malcolm sitting on a rock. He was smoking a cigar, and did not notice the approach of his friend until Strong stood before him. Then he flushed.

"Hallo, Phil," said Strong in a friendly voice which strained after a natural tone, "communing with nature?"

"No," said Malcolm; "I came up here because I was disgusted with myself. Left my buckboard on the road down there. Did you pass it?"

"I didn't notice it," answered Strong, scanning the other's face. "Look here, Phil," he went on, "I came up here to work off steam." He looked down the mountain's steep side. "You don't dare go down Newport with me?"

Malcolm pulled out his watch.

"We haven't time," he said. "It takes four hours when you have good luck. It will be dark before we strike the road."

"Will you go and risk it?" asked Strong.

"Yes," said the other, with a glance at the sinking sun.

They began the descent rapidly. They were both in the mood for hard work. As they slipped down shelving rocks or made downward leaps, catching at roots and bushes to stop their too-hurried course, their spirits lightened. They warmed to each other as in their college vacation days, when they had tramped through the White Mountains. Strong caught his foot once, and went stumbling headlong for fully twenty feet. His neck was in danger, but when Malcolm came up to him, making long jumps, the editor was laughing and panting. His cheeks were tinged, and his eyes were filled with flashing light.

"This is fine!" he said, between his heavy breathing.

"You'll break your precious neck if you do that again," said Malcolm, and laughed.

The descent became more difficult. They reached the cliff part, and it took them over an hour to make thirty yards. They were lowering themselves by inches now on jutting rocks, exposed roots, and out-hanging limbs of stunted trees. Strong was leading. He deftly slipped down to a shelf formed by the edge of a huge rock jutting out from the mountainside. Malcolm was heavier, and could not get down. Strong jammed himself close to the rocky formation and leaned over, throwing his arms around the sharp protuberances of the rock.

"Put your foot on my back, and don't kick me over the side of the cliff or we shall both be in the papers—in the obituary column," he said, laughing.

Malcolm let himself down upon Strong's back.

"Where is Atlas?" said Strong between his teeth, for Malcolm was heavy. "God, Phil!" he cried an instant later, throwing out one arm and catching Malcolm around the waist as he suddenly slipped off. "Steady, old man." Malcolm was suspended in air. Strong's muscles were like steel. He gripped the sharp rock with his left arm until the edges cut into his flesh. Bending his knees slowly, and with his teeth set, he strained down and back, dragging Malcolm up to the narrow shelf. He trembled when his arm released its hold. Malcolm was white. He looked down and shivered.

"It's getting late," said Strong, not waiting for the other to speak. "We can't go down that way," he went on hurriedly. "I have been down Newport a dozen times, and I never before got into such a box."

He looked around him. A rough line, a sort of crease, like a wrinkle in a stone face, ran along the side of the rocks.

"Stay where you are, and I will see where this leads to," said Strong.

He worked his way carefully until he disappeared around a knob of granite. Then Malcolm saw him crawling back.

"Come on," said Strong when he reached the shelf. "I guess we can make it this way."

The two felt their way, holding to the wall at their side. Malcolm was in advance.

"Here it is," said Strong, after they had turned the corner. "Now," he said, "I don't want you to be foolish, Phil. Don't object to what I am going to say. This is probably the only place on this side of the mountain which is practically impassable. We have had the bad luck to get into it. Now we can't both get out of it." He flashed a look straight into the other's eyes. Malcolm's jaw was set.

"Don't look that way," Strong said. "I know you want to stay, but that is out of the question. You could not get me down, and I can drop you as lightly as a feather. And now I am going to show you how. You see it is fifteen feet to the next place of footing. All you have to do is to land there. Now, if I lie down here," and he started to take off his coat, "and hold on to that sapling"—he kicked it with his foot—"I can swing you out far enough to drop you there. Now for it."

"I won't go," said Malcolm, doggedly. "I'll stick it out with you."

"No, you will not," answered the other. "Don't you see that it is our only hope of getting out of this? I let you down. You get shaken up, but not hurt. There, not forty yards from us, is a little ravine. That means that it is easy going there until you reach the brush. Get into the bed of the ravine, crawl under the briars, and you strike the road. You will probably meet a buckboard in the road. You can be back in two hours—three, anyway. Mark the place where you come out, get a rope and lantern, and return for me. You can throw up the rope to me, and then I am out of it."

Strong got down on his knees to carry out his program. Malcolm put his hand on his friend's shoulder to stop him.

"Wait a minute," he said. "The Colonel is to go away tomorrow morning." Strong got off his knees, but he did not answer. Malcolm also paused.

"Well?" said Strong, finally.

"Well," answered Malcolm, echoing the word, "it's just this, Fred. I did come up the mountain today to think, and I made my decision before you met me. I made up my mind to ask her tonight, and if I go down I shall go straight to her and ask her. So I refuse to go, for I know that you—besides," he broke out, "you have just saved my life."

Strong leaned against the mountainside. The sun had gone, and his shirtsleeves shone white in the dusk. He started and picked up his coat. One arm was thrust into a sleeve, when he stopped and dropped the garment again. Getting down once more, he circled the young tree with his left arm.

"Come," he said; "I will let you down."

"Very well," said Malcolm, slowly. He sat on the edge of the rocky platform. He felt Strong's arm clench him just under his two arms. He could feel the nervous strength of it as it pinned him. Then Strong pushed him gently off. As Malcolm went over the side his eye caught sight of a crimson stain on the white of Strong's sleeve where the knife-like rock had gashed him when he saved Malcolm's life.

"What's that?" cried Malcolm. "Blood?"

"Good-bye, Phil, and good luck to you," said Strong, swinging the other out, and dropping him to the firm earth below.

"This is an outrage," cried Malcolm from below. "I shall stay here. You are cut, Fred."

"Run along and get that rope. It's getting cold up here," answered Strong.

He could barely see Malcolm in the dusk as he reached the head of the ravine and turned to wave his hat. He heard an occasional crash as Malcolm beat his way through the brush; then there was silence, broken now and then by a rumble on the road far below him where some vehicle rolled along toward the town. He shivered with the chill of the approaching autumn, and buttoned his coat around his throat. He tried to follow in a mental calculation Malcolm's progress toward the town. He counted the steps he must have made, and as he thought of him getting nearer and nearer to the hotel where the Hardeservices were staying, his breath came quicker. He paced up and down on the little ledge. The cold stars were mocking him. His restless eye caught the sapling near him. He seized it and tugged at it. His hand stretched up as high as it could reach and, with the vein in the center of his forehead swelling, he bent the young tree down until he held it fast in both arms. It was over the drop. He reached out, and, shutting his eyes even in the darkness, swung clear on the swaying tree.

It sank and sank until he released his hold. He heard its hissing as it cut the air, springing erect again, and he was on the ground, shocked and stunned. He sprang to his feet and ran, half feeling his way to the spot where be knew the ravine began. He leaped, he ran, he stumbled over its uneven bed. His head was whirling, and his feet were flying. He plunged along until he reached the mass of briars. They tore his hands where he thrust them out to open a passage. They tripped his feet and pulled him to the ground. But he fought through them, impatiently and fiercely. And then he reached the road. He turned into it on a run. He ran until his feet were weighted with lead, and his lungs were choked. Nobody could see him, and nobody could hear him, and he waved his arms and burdened his lips with oaths. His ear caught the muffled beats of hoofs pounding in the dust-covered road. There was the hum of wheels before him. He crushed himself against the bushes at the roadside to let them pass. They stopped, and a light flashed in his white face. Phil's kindly eyes were peering into his. The great Colonel, who had been crying, even as the wagon approached, "To the rescue!" was tugging at his torn hand.

"Fred, old man," cried Malcolm—"Fred, how did you do it?"

Strong smiled faintly. He turned to Malcolm and gripped his hand.

"They aren't going till next week," Phil whispered in his ear.

"Great God!" cried the Colonel, "the boy is hurt. He is bleeding all over." Then he opened his lungs.

"Back to the hotel!" he roared, and the wheels went spinning toward Bar Harbor.

They were all dancing. It was the last dance of the season. The perfume of crushed flowers was in the air, and there was a hum in the room which arose above the music. You could hear words of farewell, light laughter, and pretty compliments. Malcolm and the younger Miss Hardeservice fell out from the moving throng, and went over to a corner where Mrs. Hardeservice sat admiring her two daughters. The Colonel was not there. He was up in his room framing a letter which would assist him to discount his pay in advance. Strong and Miss Hardeservice were promenading the room. Malcolm, Mrs. Hardeservice, and her younger daughter kept their eyes on them. They were a handsome couple. In Miss Hardeservice's cheek was a bright color. Her lips were parted in a half-formed smile, and her eyes sparkled under the light.

Strong's face had a light of reckless daring. Both tall and fair, many eyes followed them. Malcolm, watching them closely, showed in his face how he envied the fire and spirit of his friend. There was a look of hunger and discontent in his dark eyes. The younger Miss Hardeservice saw it, while she watched her sister. When Malcolm turned to her with a guilty start, she was slightly pale, and her fan was moving quickly. He dared not look into her soft eyes.

"Won't you go out for a promenade on the veranda?" he said.

The walking space was crowded, and they found two chairs. He wanted to say something, but his lips were treacherous. They faltered and stumbled over the words. He was comparing himself with Strong. The editor was brave and reliant. Strong would ask Bess to marry him before she left Bar Harbor. He knew that, and he felt a pang when he remembered that this was the last night. If he could only make his lips say what he wanted them to confess. It startled him when he thought how everyone fancied that he loved Eleanor. He looked at the little Miss Hardeservice in a frightened way. She was very quiet. Suddenly he bent over. Three words, and he was trembling fearfully. Something in her eyes and in the way her hand fluttered sent a flash of courage through him. The words came forth of their own will.

When they went back to Mrs. Hardeservice, Bess's olive cheek was tinted with a soft color. Strong was not about, and Eleanor had gone upstairs to her father. Mother and daughter followed her. Bess, like a shy child, entered the room where her father and Eleanor sat. The pink in her cheek had not faded, and her eyes were soft and liquid. The old soldier's face was down between his hands. Eleanor sat erect, a little pale, and her eyes were feverishly brilliant.

Bess went up to her father and curled her arm about his neck, so that her hand rested on his cheek. The Colonel sighed. Eleanor had just told him that she was going to be married to Strong. His first thought had been of Bess, and the shock stunned him. Bess crossed the room to her mother, who was smiling softly, and, leading her up to the old man, knelt at his feet. He was kissing her as they told him the truth, and Eleanor was pressing his great hand to her lips. The old Colonel sobbed like a great boy, and then smiled through his tears.

Strong meanwhile was smoking a cigar before going to bed. Malcolm came up to him. He felt guilty. The editor greeted him warmly, over-heartily. He was elated, and his manner showed it; but he had the disposition of a conqueror. He felt that he could afford to be generously kind to his friend. They had both striven for the same prize, and he had won; all honor to a noble rival who had lost.

Malcolm was embarrassed. He could scarcely believe his good fortune. He had beaten a more able man, a man whom he loved, and for whom he felt sympathy; and yet he could not grieve for the other. It was fate that he should succeed over a better man. He wanted to strengthen their friendship before the blow fell which should try it. He did not know how to begin.

Strong handed him a cigar, and tried to look serious. Malcolm's match sounded loud and out of harmony.

"Poor old Phil! how shall I tell him?" thought Strong. "It will be a great shock to him."

"I wish I had Fred's courage," Malcolm said to himself. "so that I could break it to him." And the two smoked in silence.

Ervin Wardman (1865–1923)

Ervin Wardman was born in Salt Lake City and educated at Phillips Exeter Academy and Harvard University. After his college graduation, Wardman became a reporter for the New York Tribune, *and he spent thirty-four years working for various New York newspapers, specializing in reporting economic and labor news. He took time off to serve in the Spanish-American War in 1905. His high standards for newspaper reporting led him to coin the term "yellow journalism" for his competitors that did not meet them. At the time of his death he was vice president of the* New York Sun. The New York Times *lauded his contribution to his profession: "While broad-minded and always courteously considerate of others, he had strong convictions of his own and stood up for them with entire directness and fearlessness."*

Chapter 10

Love in Idleness

Marion Crawford

1894

This is the first chapter of Love in Idleness: A Tale of Bar Harbor, *which is arguably the quintessential Bar Harbor novel. The town is seen through the eyes of a young New York artist, Louis Armstrong, who finds himself out of his league among Bostonians as he seeks to woo Fanny Trehearne. In this excerpt, the author not only sets the stage but adds a biting critique of the architecture of early Bar Harbor hotels, as well as a send-up of the pretentious social life found elsewhere on Mount Desert at the time.*

"I'm going to stay with the three Miss Minors at the Trehearnes' place," said Louis Lawrence, looking down into the blue water as he leaned over the rail of the *Sappho*, on the sunny side of the steamer. "They're taking care of Miss Trehearne while her mother is away at Karlsbad with Mr. Trehearne," he added in further explanation.

"Yes," answered Professor Knowles, his companion. "Yes," he repeated vaguely, a moment later.

"It's fun for the three Miss Minors, having such a place all to themselves for the summer," continued young Lawrence. "It's less amusing for Miss Trehearne, I daresay. I suppose I'm asked to enliven things. It can't be exactly gay in their establishment."

"I don't know any of them," observed the Professor, who was a Boston man. "The probability is that I never shall. Who are the three Miss Minors, and who is Miss Trehearne?"

"Oh—you don't know them!" Lawrence's voice expressed his surprise that there should be anyone who did not know the ladies in question. "Well—they're three old maids, you know."

"Excuse me, I don't know. *Old maid* is such a vague term. How old must a maid be, to be an old maid?"

"Oh—it isn't age that makes old maids. It's the absence of youth. They're born so."

"A pleasing paradox," remarked the Professor, his exaggerated jaw seeming to check the uneasy smile, as it attacked the gravity of his colorless thin lips.

His head, in the full face view, was not too large for his body, which, in the two dimensions of length and breadth, was well proportioned. The absence of the third dimension, that is, of bodily thickness, was very apparent when he was seen sideways, while the exaggeration of the skull was also noticeable only in profile. The forehead and the long delicate jaw were unnaturally prominent; the ear was set much too far back, and there was no development over the eyes, while the nose was small, thin, and sharp, as though cut out of letter paper.

"It's not a paradox," said Lawrence, whose respect for professorial statements was small. "The three Miss Minors were old maids before they were born. They're not particularly old, except Cordelia. She must be over forty. Augusta is the youngest—about thirty-two, I should think. Then there's the middle one—she's Elizabeth, you know—she's no particular age. Cordelia must have been pretty—in a former state. Lots of brown hair and beautiful teeth. But she has the religious smile—what they put on when they sing hymns, don't you

In the Woods.

know? It's chronic. Good teeth and resignation did it. She's good all through, but you get all through her so soon! Elizabeth's clever—comparatively. She's brown, and round, and fat and ugly. I'd like to paint her portrait. She's really by far the most attractive. As for Augusta—"

"Well? What about Augusta?" enquired the Professor, as Lawrence paused.

"Oh—she's awful! She's the accomplished one."

"I thought you said that the middle one—what's her name?—was the cleverest."

"Yes, but cleverness never goes with what they call accomplishments," answered the young man. "I've heard of great men playing the flute, but I never heard of anybody who was 'musical' and came to anything—especially women. Fancy Cleopatra playing the piano—or Catherine the Great painting a salad of wild flowers on a fan! Can you? Or Semiramis sketching a lap dog on a cushion!"

"What very strange ideas you have!" observed the Professor.

Lawrence did not say anything in reply, but looked over the blue water at the dark islands on the deep bay as the *Sappho* paddled along, beating up a wake of egg-white froth. He was glad that Professor Knowles was going over to the other side to dwell amongst the placid inhabitants of Northeast Harbor, where the joke dieth not, even at an advanced age; where there are people who believe in Ruskin and swear by Herbert Spencer, who coin words ending in 'ism,' and intellectually subsist on the 'ologies'—with the notable exception of theology. Lawrence had once sat at the Professor's feet, at Harvard, unwillingly, indeed, but not without indirect profit. They had met today in the train, and it was not probable that they should meet again in the course of the summer, unless they particularly sought one another's society.

They had nothing in common. Lawrence was an artist, or intended to be one, and had recently returned from abroad, after spending three years in Paris. By parentage he belonged to New York. He had been christened Louis because his mother was of French extraction and had an uncle of that name, who might be expected to do something handsome for her son. Louis Lawrence was now about five and twenty years of age, was possessed of considerable talent, and of no particularly worldly goods. His most important and valuable possession, indeed, was his character, which showed itself in all he said and did.

There is something problematic about the existence of a young artist who is in earnest, which alone is an attraction in the eyes of women. The odds are ten to one, of course, that he will never accomplish anything above the average, but that one-tenth chance is not to be despised, for it is the possibility of a well-earned celebrity, perhaps of greatness. The one last step, out of obscurity into fame, is generally the only one of which the public knows anything, sees anything, or understands anything; and no one can tell when, if ever, that one step may be taken. There is a constant interest in expecting it, and in knowing of its possibility, which lends the artist's life a real charm in his own eyes and the eyes of others. And very often it turns out that the charm is all the life has to recommend it.

The young man who had just given Professor Knowles an account of his hostesses was naturally inclined to be communicative, which is a weakness, though he was also frank, which is a virtue. He was a very slim young man, and might have been thought to be in delicate health, for he was pale and thin in the face. The features were long and finely chiseled, and the complexion was decidedly dark. He would have looked well in a lace ruffle, with flowing curls. But his hair was short, and he wore rough gray clothes and an unobtrusive tie. The highly arched black eyebrows gave his expression strength, but the very minute, dark mustache which shaded the upper lip was a little too evidently twisted and trained. That was the only outward sign of personal vanity, however, and was not an offensive one, though it gave him a foreign air which Professor Knowles disliked, but which the three Miss Minors thought charming. His manner pleased them, too; for he was always just as civil to them as though they had been young and pretty, and amusing, which is more than can be said of the majority of modern youths. His conversation occasionally shocked them, it is true; but the shock was a mild one and agreeably applied, so that they were willing to undergo it frequently.

Lawrence was not thinking of the Miss Minors as he watched the dark green islands. If he had thought of them at all during the last half-hour, it had been with a certain undefined gratitude to them for being the means of allowing him to spend a fortnight in the society of Fanny Trehearne.

Professor Knowles had not moved from his side during the long silence. Lawrence looked up and saw that he was still there, his extraordinary profile cut out against the cloudless sky.

"Will you smoke?" enquired Lawrence, offering him a cigarette.

"No thank you—certainly not cigarettes," answered the Professor, with a superior air. "You were telling me all about the Miss Minors," he continued; for though he knew none of them, he was of a curious disposition. "You spoke of Miss Trehearne, I think."

"Yes," answered the young man. "Do you know her?"

"Oh no. It's an unusual name, that's all. Are they New York people?"

Lawrence smiled at the idea that anyone should ask such a question.

"Yes, of course," he answered. "New York—since the Flood."

"And Miss Trehearne is the only daughter?" inquired the Professor, inquisitively.

"She has a brother—Randolph," replied Lawrence, rather shortly; for he was suddenly aware that there was no particular reason why he should talk about the Trehearnes.

"Of course, they're relations of the Minors," observed the Professor.

"That's the reason why Miss Trehearne has them to stay with her. Excuse me—I can't get a light in this wind."

Thereupon Lawrence turned away and got under the lee of the deck saloon, leaving the Professor to himself. Having lighted his cigarette, the artist went forward and stood in the sharp head-breeze that seemed to blow through and through

him, disinfecting his whole being from the hot, close air of the train he had left a half an hour earlier.

Bar Harbor, in common speech, includes Frenchman's Bay, the island of Mount Desert, and the other small islands lying near it—an extensive tract of land and sea. As a matter of fact, the name belongs to the little harbor between Bar Island and Mount Desert, together with the village which has grown to be the center of civilization, since the whole place has become fashionable. Earth, sky, water are of the north—hard, bright, and cold. In artists' slang, there is no atmosphere. The dark green islands, as one looks at them, seem to be almost before the foreground. The picture is beautiful, and some call it grand; but it lacks depth. There is something fiercely successful about the color of it, something brilliantly self-reliant. It suggests a certain type of handsome woman—of the kind that need neither repentance nor cosmetics, and are perfectly sure of the fact, whose virtue is too cold to be kind, and whose complexion is not shadowed by passion, nor softened by suffering, nor even washed pale with tears. Only the sea is eloquent. The deep-breathing tide runs forward to the feet of the over-perfect, heartless earth, to linger and plead love's story while he may; then sighing sadly, sweeps back unsatisfied, baring his desolate bosom to her loveless scorn.

The village, the chief center, lies by the water's edge, facing the islands which enclose the natural harbor. It was and is a fishing village, like many another on the coast. In the midst of it, vast wooden hotels, four times as high as the houses nearest to them, have sprung up to lodge fashion in six-storied discomfort. The effect is astonishing; for the blatant architect, gesticulating in soft wood and ranting in paint, as it were, has sketched an evil dream of medievalism, incoherent with itself and with the very commonplace facts of the village street. There, also, in Mr. Bee's shop window, are plainly visible the more or less startling covers of the newest books, while from on high, frowns down the counterfeit presentment of battlements and turrets, and of such terrors as lent like interest when novels were not, neither was the slightest idea of the short story yet conceived.

But behind all and above all rise the wooded hills, which are neither modern nor ancient, but eternal. And in them and through them there is secret sweetness, and fragrance, and much that is gentle and lovely—in the heart of the defiantly beautiful earth-woman with her cold face, far beyond the reach of her tide-lover, and altogether out of hearing of his sighs and complaining speeches. There grow in endless greenness the white pines and the pitch pines, the black spruce and the white; there droops the feathery larch by the creeping yew, and there gleam the birches, yellow, white, and gray; the sturdy red oak spreads his arms to the scarlet maple, and the witch hazel rustles softly in the mysterious forest breeze. There, buried in the wood's bosom, bloom and blossom the wild flowers, and redden the blushing berries in unseen succession, from middle June to late September—violets first, and wild iris, strawberries and raspberries, blueberries and blackberries; short-lived wild roses and tender little bluebells, red lilies, goldenrod, and clematis, in the confusion of nature's loveliest order.

All this Lawrence knew, and remembered, guessing at that he could neither remember nor know, with an artist's facility for filling up the unfinished sketch left on the mind by one impression. He had been at Bar Harbor three years earlier, and had wandered amongst the woods and pottered along the shore in a skiff. But he had been alone then and had stopped in the medieval hotel, a rather solitary, thinking unit amidst the horde of thoughtless summer nomads, designated by the clerk at the desk as "Number a hundred and twenty-three," and a candidate for a daily portion of the questionable dinner at the hotel table. It was to be different this time, he thought, as he watched for the first sight of the pier when the *Sappho* rounded Bar Island. The Trehearnes had not been at their house three years ago, and Fanny Trehearne had been then not quite sixteen, groping her way from the schoolroom to the world, and quite beneath his young importance—even had she been at Bar Harbor to wander among the woods with him. Things had changed, now. He was not quite sure that in her girlish heart she did not consider him beneath her notice. She was straight and tall—almost as tall as he, and she was proud, if she was not pretty, and she carried her head as high as the handsomest. Moreover, she was rich, and Louis Lawrence was at present phenomenally poor, with a rather distant chance of inheriting money. These were some of the excellent reasons why fate had made him fall in love with her, though none of them accounted for the fact that she had encouraged him, and had suggested to the Miss Minors that it would be very pleasant to have him come and stay a fortnight in July.

The *Sappho* slowed down, stopped, backed, and made fast to the wooden pier, and as she swung round, Lawrence saw Fanny Trehearne standing a little apart from the group of people who had come down to meet their own friends or to watch other people meeting theirs. The young girl was evidently looking for him, and he took off his hat and waved it about erratically to attract her attention. When she saw him, she nodded with a faint smile and moved one step nearer to the gangway, to wait until he should come on shore with the crowd.

She had a quiet, businesslike way of moving, as though she never changed her position without a purpose. As Lawrence came along, trying to gain on the stream of passengers with whom he was moving, he kept his eyes fixed on her face, wondering whether the expression would change when he reached her and took her hand. When the moment came, the change was very slight.

"I like you—you're punctual," she said. "Come along!"

"I've got some traps, you know," he answered, hesitating.

"Well—there's the expressman. Give him your checks."

Marion Crawford (1854–1909)

Marion Crawford was born in Italy to American parents; his father, Thomas Crawford, was a well-known sculptor and his mother, Louisa Ward, was a sister of Julia Ward Howe. After studying in the United States, England, and Germany, he became a journalist and novelist, living in New York and Boston before returning to Italy in 1883. Among his other novels are Mr. Isaacs *(1882),* Dr. Claudius *(1883), and* A Roman Singer *(1884). His novels, most with Italian settings, have vivid characterizations and settings.*

Chapter 11

On Frenchman's Bay

Constance C. Harrison
1895

Convinced that he has a mysterious terminal illness, a young man invites his unsuspecting wife and his best friend to join him for a holiday in Bar Harbor. The delights of the resort, both natural and man-made, nearly cause him to forget about his gloomy future. This is the third of Constance Harrison's Bar Harbor stories. It was originally published in the author's collection, A Virginia Cousin and Bar Harbor Tales *(Boston: Lamson, Wolffe and Co., 1895, pp. 145–202).*

I

From Maxwell Pollock, Esq., No.—Firth Avenue, New York, to Stephen Cranbrooke, Esq.—Club, New York.

May 30, 189—,

My dear Cranbrooke:

You will wonder why I follow up our conversation of last evening with a letter; why, instead of speaking, I should write what is left to be said between us two.

But after a sleepless night, of which my little wife suspects nothing, I am impelled to confide in you—my oldest friend, her friend, although you and she have not yet grown to the comprehension of each other I hoped for when she married me three years ago—a secret that has begun to weigh heavily upon my soul.

I do not need to remind you that, since our college days, you have known me subject to fits of moodiness and depression upon which you have often rallied me. How many times you have said that a fellow to whom Fate had given health, strength, opportunity, and fortune—and recently the treasury of a lovely and loving wife—has no business to admit the word "depression" into his vocabulary!

This is true. I acknowledge it, as I have a thousand times before. I am a fool, a coward, to shrink from what is before me. But I was still more of a fool and a coward when I married her. For her sake, the prospect of my death before this summer wanes, impels me to own to you my certainty that my end is close at hand.

In every generation of our family since the old fellow who came over from England and founded us on Massachusetts soil, the oldest son has been snatched out of life upon the threshold of his thirtieth year. I carried into college with me an indelible impression of the sudden and distressing death of my father, at that period of his prosperous career, and of the wild cry of widowed mother when she clasped me to her breast, and prayed Heaven might avert the doom from me.

Everything that philosophy, science, common sense, could bring to the task of arguing me out of a belief in the transmission of this sentence of a higher power to me, has been tried. I have studied, traveled, lived, enjoyed myself in a rational way; have loved and won the one woman upon earth for me, have reveled in her wifely tenderness.

I have tried to do my duty as a man and a citizen. In all other respects, I believe myself to be entirely rational, coolheaded, unemotional; but I have never been able to down that specter. He is present at every feast; and although in perfectly good health, I resolved yesterday to put the question to a practical test. I called at the office of an eminent specialist, whom I had never met, although doubtless he knew my name, as I knew his.

Joining the throng of waiting folk in Dr. ——'s outer office, I turned over the leaves of the last number of Punch, with what grim enjoyment of its menu of jocularity you may conceive. When my turn came, I asked for a complete physical examination. But the doctor got no farther than my heart before I was conscious of awakening interest on his part. When the whole business was over, he told me frankly that in what he was pleased to call "a magnificent physique," there was but one blemish—a spot upon the ripe side of a peach—a certain condition of the heart that "might or might not" give serious trouble in the future.

"Might or might not"! How I envied the smooth-spoken man of science his ability to say these words so glibly! While I took his medical advice—that, between us, was not worth a straw, and he knew it, and I knew it—I was thinking of Ethel. I saw her face when she should know the worst, and I became, immediately, an abject, cringing, timorous thing, that crept out of the doctor's office into the spring sunshine, wondering why the world was all a-cold.

Here's where the lash hits me: I should never have married Ethel; I should, knowing my doom, have married no one but some commonplace, platitudinous creature, whom the fortune I shall leave behind would have consoled. But Ethel! High-strung, ardent, simple-hearted, worshipping me far beyond my deserts! Why did I condemn her, poor girl, to what is so soon to come?

On the fifteenth day of the coming August, I shall have reached thirty years. Before that day, the blow will fall upon her, and it is all my fault. You know, Cranbrooke, that I do not fear death. What manly soul fears death? It is only to the very young, or to the very weak of spirit, the King appears in all his terrors. Having expected him so long and so confidently, I hope I may meet him with a courageous front. But Ethel! Ethel!

She will be quite alone with me this summer. Her mother and sisters have just sailed for the other side, and I confess I am selfish enough to crave her to myself in the last hours. But someone she must have to look after her, and whom can I trust like you? I want you to promise me to come to us to spend your August holiday; to be there, in fact, when—

In the meantime, there must be no suggestion of what I expect. She, least of all, must suspect it. I should like to go out to the unknown with her lighthearted, girlish laugh ringing in my ears.

When we meet, as usual, you will oblige me by saying nothing of this letter or its contents. By complying with this request, you will add one more—a final one, dear old man—to the long list of kindnesses for which I am your debtor; and believe me, dear Cranbrooke,

Yours, always faithfully,
Maxwell Pollock

"Good heavens!" exclaimed Stephen Cranbrooke, dropping the sheet as if it burnt him, and sitting upright and aghast. "So *this* is the cranny in Pollock's brain where I have never before been able to penetrate."

Later that day, Mr. Cranbrooke received another epistle, prefaced by the house address of the Maxwell Pollocks.

"Dear Mr. Cranbrooke," this letter ran, "Max tells me he has extended to you an invitation to share our solitude *à deux* in your August holiday. I need hardly say that I endorse this heartily; and I hope you will not regret to learn that, instead of going, as usual, to our great big isolated country place in New Hampshire, I have persuaded Max to take a cottage on the shore of Frenchman's Bay, near Bar Harbor—but not too near that gay resort—where he can have his sailboat and canoe, and a steam launch for me to get about in. They say the sunsets over the water there are adorable, and Max has an artist's soul, as you know, and will delight in the picturesque beauty of it all.

"I want to tell you, confidentially, that I have fancied a change of air and scene might do him good this year. He is certainly not ill; but is, as certainly, not himself. I suppose you will think I am a little goose for saying so; but I believe if anything went wrong with Max, I could never stand up against it. And there is no other man in the world, than you, whom I would ask to help me find out what it really is that worries him—whether ill-fortune, or what—certainly not ill-health, for his is a model of splendid vigor, as everybody knows, my beautiful husband!"

"This is what she calls pleasant reading for me," said plain, spare Stephen Cranbrooke, with a whimsical twist of his expressive mouth.

"At any rate," he read, resuming, "you and I will devote ourselves to making it nice for him up there. No man, however he loves his wife, can afford to do altogether without men's society; and it is so hard for me to get Max to go into general company, or to cultivate intimacy with any man but you!

"There is a bachelor's wing to the cottage we have taken, with a path leading direct to the wharf where the boats are moored; and this you can occupy by yourself, having breakfast alone, as Max and I are erratic in that respect. We shall have a buckboard for the ponies, and our saddle horses, with a horse for you to ride; and we shall pledge each other not to accept a single invitation to anybody's house, unless it pleases us to go there.

"Not less than a month will we take from you, and I wish it might be longer. Perhaps you may like to know there is no other man Max would ask, and I should want, to be 'one of us' under such circumstances.

"Always cordially yours.
"Ethel Pollock"

"I asked her for bread, and she gave me a stone," he quoted, with a return of the whimsical expression. "Well! Neither he nor she has ever suspected my infatuation. I am glad she wrote me though, for it makes the watch I mean to set over Max easier. After looking at his case in every respect, I am convinced there is a remedy, if I can only find it."

A knock, just then, at the door of Mr. Cranbrooke's comfortable bachelor sitting room was followed by the appearance of a man, at sight of whom Cranbrooke's careworn and puzzled countenance brightened perceptibly.

"Ha! Shepard!" he said, rising to bestow on the newcomer a hearty grip of the hand. "Did you divine how much I wanted to talk to a fellow who has pursued exactly your line of study, and one, too, who, more than any other I happen to be acquainted with, knows just how far mind may be made to influence matter in preventing catastrophe, when—but, there, what am I to do? It's another man's affair—a confidence that must be held inviolable."

"Give me the case hypothetically," said Shepard, dropping, according to custom, into a leathern chair out at elbows but full of comfort to the spine of reclining man, while accepting one of Cranbrooke's galaxy of famously tinted pipes.

"I think I will try to do so," rejoined his friend, "since upon it hangs the weal or woe of two people, in their way more interesting to me than any others in the world."

"I am all ears," said Dr. Shepard, fixing upon Cranbrooke the full gaze of a pair of deep-set orbs that had done their full share of looking intelligently into the mystery of cerebral vagaries. Cranbrooke, as well as he could, told the gist of Pollock's letter, expressing his opinion that to a man of the writer's temperament the conviction of approaching death was as good as an actual death warrant.

Shepard, who asked nothing better than an intelligent listener when launched upon his favorite theories, kept the floor for fifteen minutes in a brilliant offhand discourse full of technicalities intermingled with sallies of strong original thought, to which Cranbrooke listened, as men in such a case are wont to do, in fascinated silence.

"But this is generalizing," the doctor interrupted himself at last. "What you want is a special discussion of your friend's condition. Of course, not knowing his physical state, I can't pretend to say how long it is likely to be before that heart trouble will pull him up short. But the merest tyro knows that men under sentence from heart disease have lived their full life span. It is the obsession of his mind, the invasion of his nerves by that long-brooding idea, that bothers me. I am inclined to think the odds are he will go mad if he doesn't die."

"Good God, Shepard!" came from his friend's pale lips.

"Isn't that what you were worrying about when I came in? Yes—you needn't answer. You think so, too; and we are not posing as wise men when we arrive at that simple conclusion."

"What on earth are we to do for him?"

"I don't know, unless it be to distract his mind by some utterly unlooked-for concatenation of circumstances. Get his wife to make love to another man, for instance."

"Shepard, you forget; these are my nearest friends."

"And you forget I am a skeptic about a love between the sexes that cannot be alienated," answered the little doctor, coolly.

Cranbrooke had indeed, for a moment, lost sight of his confidant's dark page of life—forgotten the experience that, years ago, had broken up the doctor's home, and made of him a scoffer against the faith of woman. He was silent, and Shepard went on with no evidence of emotion.

"When that happened to *me*, it was a dynamite explosion that effectually broke up the previous courses of thought within me; and, naturally, the idea occurs to me as a specific case of your melancholy friend. Seriously, Cranbrooke, you could do worse than attack him from some unexpected quarter, in some point where he is acutely sensitive—play upon him, excite him, distract him, and so carry him past the date he fears."

"How could I?" asked Cranbrooke of himself.

There was another knock; and, upon Cranbrooke's hearty bidding to come in, there entered no less a person than the subject of their conversation.

Even the astute Shepard finished his pipe and took his leave without suspecting that the manly, healthy, clear-eyed, and animated Maxwell Pollock had anything in common with the hero of Cranbrooke's story. Cranbrooke, who had dreaded a reopening of the subject of Pollock's letter, was infinitely relieved to find it left untouched.

The visit, lasting till past midnight, was one of a long series dating back to the time when they were undergraduates at the university. There had never been a break in their friendship. The society of Cranbrooke, after that of his wife, was to Pollock ever the most refreshing, the most inspiring to high and manly thought. They talked, now, upon topics grave and gay, without hinting at the shadow overlying all. Pollock was at his best; and his friend's heart went out to him anew in a way of that sturdy affection "passing the love of a woman"—rare, perhaps, in our material, money-getting community, but, happily, still existing among true men.

When the visitor arose to take leave, he said in simple fashion: "Then I may count on you, Cranbrooke, to stand by us this summer?"

"Count on me in all things," Cranbrooke answered; and the two shook hands, and Pollock went his way cheerily, as usual.

"Is this a dream?" Cranbrooke asked himself, when left alone. "Can it be possible that sane, splendid fellow is a victim of pitiful hallucination, or that he is really to be cut off in the golden summer of his days? No, it can't be; it must not be. He must be, as Shepard says, 'pulled up short' by main force. At any cost, I must save him. But how? *Anyhow*! Max must be made to forget himself—even if I am the sacrifice! But George! This *is* a plight I'm in! And Ethel, who adores the ground he walks upon! I shall probably end by losing both of them, worse luck!"

The morning had struggled through Cranbrooke's window blinds before he stirred from his fit of musing and went into his bedroom for a few hours of troubled sleep.

II

Mr. and Mrs. Pollock took possession of their summer abiding place on a glorious day of refulgent June, such as, in the dazzling atmosphere of Mount Desert Island, makes every more southerly resort on our Atlantic coast seem dull by comparison. To greet them, they found a world of fresh-washed young birches sparkling in the sun; of spice-distilling evergreens, cropping up between gray rocks; of staring white marguerites, and huge, yellow, satin buttercups, ablow in all the clearings; of crisp, young ferns and blue iris, unfolding amid the greenery of the wilder bits of island; haunts that were soon, in turn, to be blushing pink with a miracle of briar roses.

And what a charmed existence followed! In the morning, they awoke to see the water, beneath their windows, sparkle red in the track of the rising sun; the islets blue-black in the intense glow. All day they lived abroad in the virgin woods, or on the bay in their canoe. And, after sunsets of radiant beauty, they would fall asleep, lulled by the lapping of little waves upon the rock girdle that bound their lawn. It was all lovely, invigorating, healthful. Of the cottagers who composed the summer settlement, only those had arrived there who, like the Pollocks, wanted chiefly to be to themselves.

In these early days of the season, Max and Ethel liked to explore on horseback the bosky roads that thread the island, startling the mother partridge, crested and crafty, from her nest, or sending her, in affected woe, in a direction to lead one away from where her brood was left; lending themselves to the pretty comedy with smiles of sympathy. Or else, they would rifle the ferny combs of dew-laden blossoms, all the while hearkening to the spring chatter of birds that did their best to give utterance to what wind-voice and leaf-tone failed to convey to human comprehension. Then, emerging from green arcades, our equestrians would find themselves, now, in some rocky haunt of primeval solitude facing lonely hilltops and isolated tarns; now, gazing upon a stretch of laughing sea framed by a cleft in the highlands.

Another day, they would climb on foot to some higher mountaintop, and there, whipped by tonic breezes, stand looking down upon the wooded waves of lesser summits, inland; and, seaward, to the broad Atlantic, with the ships; and, along the coast, to the hundreds of fiords, with their burden of swirling waters!

Coming home from these morning expeditions with spirit refreshed and appetite sharpened, it was their custom to repair, after luncheon, to the water, and by the aid of sails, steam, or their own oars or paddles, cut the sapphire bay with tracks of argent brightness, or linger for many a happy hour in the green shadow of the sylvan shore.

The month of July was upon the wane before husband and wife seemingly aroused to the recollection that their idyl was about to be interrupted by the invasion of a third person.

Ethel, indeed, had pondered regretfully upon the coming of Cranbrooke for some days before she spoke of it to her husband; while Max—

The real purpose of Cranbrooke's visit, dismissed from Pollock's mind with extraordinary success during the earlier weeks of their stay upon the island, had by now assumed, in spite of him, the suggestion of a deathwatch set upon a prisoner. He strove not to think of it. He refrained from speaking of it. So delicious had been to him the draft of Ethel's society, uninterrupted by outsiders, in this Eden of the eastern sea; so perfect their harmony of thought and speech; so charming her beauty, heightened by salt air and outdoor exercise and early hours, Max wondered if the experience had been sent to him as an especial allowance of mercy to the condemned. To the very day of Cranbooke's arrival, even after a trap had been sent to the evening boat to fetch him, the husband and wife refrained from discussing the expected event.

It was the hour before sunset, following a showery afternoon; and, standing together upon their lawn to look at the western sky, Max proposed to her to go out with him for a while in the canoe. They ran like children, hand in hand, to the wharf, where, lifting the frail birch-bark craft from its nest, he set it lightly afloat. Ethel, stepping expertly into her place, was followed by Max, who, in his loose cheviot shirt, bare-armed and bareheaded, flashing his red-dyed paddle in the clear water, seemed to her the embodiment of manly grace and strength.

They steered into the bay; and, as they paused to look back upon the shore, the glory of the scene grew to be unspeakable. Beyond the village, over which the electric globes had not yet begun to gleam, toward Newport, a rampart of glowing bronze, arched by a rainbow printed upon a brooding cloud. Elsewhere, the multicolored sky flamed with changing hues, reflected in a sea of glass. And out of this sea arose wooded islands; and, far on the opposite shore of the mainland, the triple hills had put on a vestment of deepest royal purple.

"I like to look away from the splendor, to the side that is in the shadow," said Ethel. "See, along that eastern coast, how the reflected sunlight is flashed from the windows on that height, and the blue columns of hearth smoke arise from the chimneys! Doesn't it make you somehow rejoice that, when the color fades, as it soon must, we shall still have our home and the lights we make for ourselves to go back to?"

There was a long silence.

"What has set you to moralizing, dear?" he asked, trying to conceal that he had winced at her innocent question.

"Oh! Nothing. Only, when one is supremely happy, as I am now, one is afraid to believe that it will endure. How mild the air is tonight! Look over yonder, Max; the jeweled necklace of Sorrento's lights has begun to palpitate. Let us paddle around that fishing schooner before we turn."

"Ethel, you are crying."

"Am I? Then it is for pure delight. I think, Max, we had never so fine an inspiration as that of coming to Mount Desert. My idea of the place has always been of a lot of rantipole gaieties, and people crowded into hotels. While this—it is a little like Norway, and a great deal like Southern Italy. Besides, when before have we been so completely to ourselves as in that gray stone lodge by the waterside, with its hood of green ivy, and the green hill rising behind it? Let us come every year; better still, let us build ourselves a summer home upon these shores."

"Should you like me to buy the cottage we now have, so that you can keep it to come to when you like?"

"When *you* like, you mean. Max, it can't be you have caught cold in this soft air, but your voice sounds a little hoarse. Well! I suppose we must go in, for Mr. Cranbrooke will be arriving very soon."

Ethel's sigh found an echo in one from her husband, at which the April-natured young woman laughed.

"There, it's out! We don't want even Cranbrooke, do we? To think the poor, dear man's coming should have been oppressing both of us, and neither would be first to acknowledge it! After all, Max, it is your fault. It was you who proposed Cranbrooke. I knew, all along, that I'd be better satisfied with you alone. Now, we must just take the consequence of your overhasty hospitality, and make him as happy as we are—if we can."

"If we can!" said Max; and she saw an almost pathetic expression drift across his face—an expression that bewildered her.

"Why do you look so rueful over him?"

"I am thinking, perhaps, how hard it will be for him to look at happiness through another man's eyes."

"Nonsense! Mr. Cranbrooke is quite satisfied with his own lot. He is one of those self-contained men who could never really love, I think," said Mrs. Pollock, conclusively.

"He has in some way failed to show you his best side. He has the biggest, tenderest heart! I wish there was a woman fit for him, somewhere. But Stephen will never marry, now, I fear. She who gets him will be lucky—he is a very tower of strength to those who lean on him."

"As far as strength goes, Max, you could pick him up with your right hand. It may be silly, but I do love your size and vigor; when I see you in a crowd of average men, I exult in you. Imagine any woman who could get you wanting a thin, sallow person like Cranbrooke!"

"He can be fascinating, when he chooses," said Max.

"The best thing about Cranbrooke, Max, is that he loves you," answered his wife, wilfully.

"Then I want you, henceforth, to try to like him better, dear; to like him for himself. He is coming in answer to my urgent request; and I feel certain the more you know of him, the more you will trust in him. At any rate, give him as much of your dear self as I can spare, and you will be sure of pleasing me."

"Max, now I believe it is you who are crying, because you are too happy. I never heard such a solemn cadence in your voice. I don't want a minute of this lovely time to be sad. When we were in town, I fancied you were down—about something; now, you are yourself again; let me be happy without alloy. I am determined to be the *cigale* of the French fable, and dance and sing away the summer. Between us, we may even succeed in making that sober Cranbrooke a reflection of us both. There, now, the light has faded; quicken your speed; we must go ashore and meet him. See, the moon has risen—Oh, Max darling, to please me, paddle in that silver path!"

This was the Ethel her husband liked to see—a child in her quick variations of emotion, a woman in steadfast tenderness. Conquering his own strongly excited feeling, he smiled on her indulgently; and when, their landing reached, Cranbrooke's tall form was descried coming down the bridge to receive them, he was able to greet his friend with an unshadowed face.

The three went in to dinner, which Ethel, taking advantage of the soft, dry air, had ordered to be served in a *loggia* opening upon the water. The butler, a sympathetic Swede, had decked their little round table with wild roses in shades of shell pink, deepening to crimson. The candles, burning under pale green shades, were scarcely stirred by the faint breeze. Hard, indeed, to believe that, upon occasion, that couchant monster, the bay, could break up into huge waves, ramping shoreward, leaping over the rock wall, upon the lawn, up to the *loggia* floor, and there beat for admission to the house, upon storm shutters hastily erected to meet its onslaught!

Tonight, a swinging lantern of wrought iron sent down through its panels of opal glass a gentle illumination upon three well-pleased faces gathered around the dainty little feast.

Ethel, who, in the days of gypsying, would allow no toilets of ceremony, retained her sailor hat, with the boat gown of white serge, in which her infantile beauty showed to its best advantage. Cranbrooke was dazzled by the new bloom upon her face, the new light in her eye.

Pollock, too, tall, broad-shouldered, blond, clean-shaven save for a mustache, his costume of white flannel enhancing duly the transparent healthiness of his complexion, looked wonderfully well—so Cranbrooke thought and said.

"Does he not?" cried Ethel, exultingly. "I knew you would think so. Max has been reconstructed since we have lived outdoors in this wonderful air. Just wait, Mr. Cranbrooke, till we have done with you, and you, too, will be blossoming like the rose."

"I, that was a desert, you would say," returned Cranbrooke, smiling. Involuntarily it occurred to him to contrast his own outer man with that of his host. Somehow or other, the fond, satisfied look Ethel bestowed upon her lord aroused anew in their friend an old, teasing spirit of envy of nature's bounty to another, denied of him.

As the moon transmuted to silver the stretch of water east of them, and the three sat over the table, with its carafes and decanters and eggshell coffee cups, till the flame of a cigar-lighter died utterly in its silver beak, their talk touching all subjects pleasantly, Cranbrooke persuaded himself he had indeed been dreaming a bad dream. The journey thither, of which every mile had been like the link of a chain, was, for him, after all, a mere essay at pleasure seeking. He had come on to spend a jolly holiday with a couple of the nicest people in the world—nothing more! His fancies, his plans, his devices, conceived in sore distress of spirit, were relegated to the world of shadows, whence they had been summoned.

When Ethel left the two men for the night, and the butler came out to collect his various belongings, Pollock rose and bade Cranbrooke accompany him to see the mountains from the other side of the house. Here, turning their backs on the enchantment of the water view, they looked up at an amphitheater of hills, dominated in turn by rocky summits gleaming in the moon. But for the lap of the water upon the coast, the stir of fresh wind arising to whisper to the leaves of a clump of birches, Mother Earth around them was keeping a silent vigil.

"What a perfect midsummer night!" said Cranbrooke, drawing a deep breath of enjoyment. "After the heat and dust of that three hundred miles of railway journey from Boston, this *is* a reward!"

"We chose better than we knew the scene of my euthanasia," answered Pollock, without a tremor in his voice.

A thrill ran through Cranbrooke's veins. He could have sworn the air had suddenly become chill, as if an iceberg had floated into the bay. He tried to respond, and found himself babbling words of weak conventionality; and all the while the soul of the strong man within him was saying: "It must not be. It shall not be. If I live, I shall rescue you from this ghastly phantom."

"Don't think it necessary to give words to what you feel for me," said Pollock, smiling slightly. "You are not making a brilliant success of it, old man, and you'd better stop. And don't suppose I mean to continue to entertain my guest by lugubrious discussions of my approaching finale. Only, it is necessary that you should know several things, since the event may take us unawares. I have made you my executor, and Ethel gets all there is; that's the long and short of my will, properly signed, attested, and deposited with my lawyer before I left town. Ethel's mother and sisters will be returning to Newport in a fortnight, and they will, no doubt, come to the poor child when she needs them. There *must* be some compensation for a decree of this kind, and I have it in the absolute bliss I have enjoyed since we came here. That child-wife of mine is the most enchanting creature in the world. If I were not steeped in selfishness, I could wish she loved me a little less. But all emotions pass, and even Ethel's tears will dry."

"Good heavens, Max, you are talking like a machine! One would think this affair of yours certain. Who are you, to dare to penetrate the mystery of the decrees of your Maker—"

"None of that, if you please, Cranbrooke," interrupted Pollock; "I have fought every inch of the way along there, by myself, and have been conquered by my conviction. Did I tell you that my father, before me, struggled with similar remonstrances from *his* friends? The parson even brought bell and book to exorcise his tormentors—and all in vain. He was snuffed out in full health, and I shall be, and why should I whine at following him? Come, my dear fellow, I am keeping you out of a capital bed, from sleep you must require. There's but one matter in which you can serve me—take Ethel into your care. Win her fullest confidence; let her know that when I am not there, *you will be*."

Cranbrooke went to his room, but not to rest. When his friends next saw him, he was returning from a solitary cruise about the bay in a catboat Pollock kept at anchor near their wharf.

"Why, Mr. Cranbrooke!" cried Ethel, lightly. "That boatman says you have been out ever since daybreak. But that we espied the boat tacking about beyond that far rock, I should have been for sending in search of you."

"Cranbrooke is an accomplished sailor," said Max. "But just now, breakfast's the thing for him, Ethel. See that he is well fed, while I stroll out to the stable and look after the horses."

As he crossed the greensward, Ethel's gaze followed him, till he disappeared between a clump of trees. Then she turned to her guest.

"Let me serve you with all there is, until they bring you something hot," she said, with her usual half-flippant consideration of him. "Do you know you look very seedy? I have, for my part, no patience with these early morning exploits."

"If you could have seen the world awakening as I saw it, this morning, you would condone my offense," he answered, a curious expression Ethel thought she had detected in his eyes leaving them unclouded as he spoke.

III

No one who knew Stephen Cranbooke well could say he did anything by halves. In the days that followed his arrival at Mount Desert, Max Pollock saw that his friend was lending every effort to the task of establishing friendly relations with his wife. From her first half-petulant, half-cordial manner with him—the manner of a woman who tries to please her husband by recognition of the claim of his nearest male intimate—Ethel had passed to the degree of manifestly welcoming Cranbrooke's presence, both when with her husband and without him.

As Max saw this growing friendship, he strove to increase it by absenting himself from Ethel, instead of, as heretofore, spending every hour he could wring from the society of other folk, in the light of her smiles. His one wish that Ethel might be insensibly led to find another than himself companionable; that she might be, though never so little, weaned from her absolute dependence upon him for daily happiness, before the blow fell that was to plunge her into darkest night, kept him content in these acts of self-sacrifice.

But as was inevitable, his manner toward them both underwent a trifling change. His old buoyancy of affection was succeeded by a quiet, at times wistful, recognition of the fact that his friend and his wife had now found another interest besides himself. But he was proud to see Cranbrooke had justified his boast that he "could be fascinating when he chose"; and he was glad to think Cranbrooke at last realized the charm Ethel, apparently a mere bright bubble upon the tide of society, had to a man of intellect and heart. "It was as I said," the poor fellow reasoned to himself, trying to find comfort in the realization of his prescience; and when Ethel, alone with him, would break into pæons of his friend, and wonder how she could have been so blind to the "real man" before, Max answered her loyally that his highest wish for both of them was at last gratified.

Then the day came when there was a question of a companion for Ethel in a sailing party to which she had accepted an invitation—and for Max was destined an emotion something like distaste.

They were sitting over the breakfast table—a meal no longer exclusive to wife and husband, as had been agreed, but shared by Cranbrooke with due regularity—when Ethel broached the subject.

"You know, Max, I was foolish enough to promise that irresistible Mrs. Clayton—when she would not take no for an answer, yesterday—that *some* of us would join her water party today. It is to be an idle cruise, with no especial aim—luncheon on board their schooner-yacht; the sort of thing I knew would bore you to extinction—being huddled up with the same people half the day."

"It is the opening wedge—if you go to this, you will be booked for others, that's all," said Max, preparing to say, in a martyrized way, that he would accompany her, if she liked.

"Oh, I knew you would feel that; and so I told her she must really excuse my husband, but that I had no doubt Mr.

Cranbrooke would accept with pleasure. You see, Mr. Cranbrooke, what polite inaccuracies you are pledged by friendship to sustain."

"I *will* accept with pleasure," Stephen said, with what Max thought almost unnecessary readiness.

"Bravo!" cried Ethel. "This is the hero's spirit. And so, Max dear, you will have a long day to yourself while I am experimenting in fashionable pleasuring, and Mr. Cranbrooke is representing you in keeping an eye on me."

"You will, of course, be at home to dinner?" said her husband.

"Surely. Unless breezes betray us, and we are driven to support exhausted nature upon hardtack and champagne; for, of course, all of the Claytons' luncheon will be eaten up, and there are no stores aboard a craft like that. Will you order the buckboard for ten, dear? We rendezvous at the boat wharf. And, as there is no telling when we shall be in, don't trouble to send to meet me. Mr. Cranbrooke and I will pick up a trap to return in."

Max saw them off in the buckboard; and, as Ethel turned at some little distance and looked back at him, where he stood still on the gravel before the vine-wreathed portal, waving her hand with a charming grace, then settling again to a *tête-à-tête* with Cranbrooke, he felt vaguely resentful at being left behind.

The clear, dazzling atmosphere, the sense of youthful vitality in his being, made him repel the idea of exclusion from any function in the animated world. He almost thought Ethel should have given him a chance to say whether or no he would accompany her. Was it not, upon her part, even a bit—a *very* little bit, lacking in proper wifely feeling, to be so prompt in dispensing with his society, to accept that of others for a whole, long, bright summer's day of pleasuring?

This suggestion he put away from him as quickly as it came. He was like a spoiled child, he said to himself, who does not expect to be taken at his word. Ethel well knew his dislike of gossiping groups of idle people; equally well she remembered, no doubt, his frequent requests that she would mingle more with the world, take more pleasure on her own account. And Cranbrooke—dear old Cranbrooke—of course he was ready to punish himself by going off on such a party, when it was an opportunity to serve his friend!

So Max put his discontent away, and, mounting his horse, went off alone for a ride half around the island, lunching at Northeast Harbor, and returning, through devious ways, by nightfall.

Restored to healthy enjoyment of all things by his day in the saddle, he turned into the avenue leading to their house, buoyed up by the sweet hope of Ethel returned—Ethel on the watch for him. Already, he saw in fancy the gleam of her jaunty white yachting costume between the tubs of flowering hydrangeas ranged on either side the walk before their door. The lamps inside—the "home lights," of which she had once fondly spoken of him—were already lighted. She would, perhaps, be worrying at his delay. He quickened his speed, and rode down the avenue to the house at a brisk trot. The groom, who, from the stable, had heard the horse's feet, started up out of the shrubbery to meet him. But there was no other indication of a watch upon the movements of the master of the house.

"Mrs. Pollock has not returned, then?" he asked, conscious of blankness in his tone.

"No sir; not yet. Our orders were, not to send for her, sir, as there was no knowing when the party would get in."

"Yes, the breeze has pretty much died out since sunset," said Pollock, endeavoring to mask his disappointment by commonplace.

He went indoors; and the house, carefully arranged though it was, with flowers and furniture disposed by expert hands to greet the returning of the master, seemed to him dull and chill.

He ordered a cup of tea for himself, and, bending down, put a match to the little fire of birchwood always kept laid upon the hearth of their picturesque hall sitting room.

In a moment, the curling wreathes of pale azure that arose upon the pyre of silvery-barked logs was succeeded by a generous flame. The peculiarly sweet flavor of the burning birch was distilled upon the air. Sipping the cup of tea, as he stood in his riding clothes before the fire, Max felt a consoling warmth invade his members and expand his heart.

"They will be in directly," he said, "and, by George, I shall be as ready for my dinner as they for theirs."

In one corner of the hall stood a tall, slender-necked vase, where he had that morning watched Ethel arranging a sheaf of goldenrod with brown-seeded marshgrasses—a combination her touch had made individual and artistic to a striking degree. He recalled how, as she had finished it, she looked around, calling him and Stephen from their newspapers to admire her handiwork. He, the husband, had admired it lazily from his divan of cushions in the corner. Cranbrooke had gone over to stand beside his hostess, and then they passed, still in close conversation, out to the grassy terrace above the sea.

Now, why should this recollection awaken in Max Pollock a new sense of the feeling he had been doing his best to dispose of all day? He could not say; but there it was, to prick him with its invisible sting. Then, too, the dinner hour was past, and he was hungry.

He went out upon the veranda at the rear, and surveyed the expanse of water. Far off, between the electric ball that hung over the wharf of the village, and the point of Bar Island, opposite, he saw a bridge of lights from yachts of all sorts, with which the harbor was now full. He fancied a little moving star of light, that seemed to creep beneath the large ones, might be the Claytons' boat on her return, and, after another interval of watching, called up a wharf authority by telephone, and asked if the *Lorelei* was in.

"Not yet, sir," was the reply. "Probably caught out when the wind fell. Will let you know the minute they are in sight." With which assurance Mr. Pollock was finally driven by the pangs of natural appetite to sit down alone to a cheerless meal.

There was a message by telephone, as he finished his repast. The *Lorelei* was in, and Mrs. Pollock desired to speak to her husband.

"We're all right," Ethel's voice said, "and I hope you haven't been worried. They *insist* on our going to dinner at a restaurant, and, of course, you understand, I can't spoil the fun by refusing. *Couldn't* you come down and meet us?"

His first impulse was to say yes; but a second thought withheld him. He gave her a pleasant answer, however, bidding her enjoy herself without thought of him, and adding: "Cranbrooke will look out for you and bring you home."

It was quite ten o'clock when they arrived at the cottage, Ethel in high spirits, flushed with the excitement of a merry day, full of chatter over people and things Max had no interest in, appealing to Cranbrooke to enjoy her retrospects with her. She was "awfully sorry" about having kept Max from his dinner; "awfully sorry" not to have come home at once, but there was no getting out of the impromptu dinner; and of course, they had to wait for it; and she was the first, after dinner, to make the move to go; Mr. Cranbrooke would certify to that.

"I don't need any certification, dear," said Max, gently; but he did not smile. Cranbrooke, who sat with him after sleepy Ethel had retired from the scene, felt his heart wrung at the thought of certain things that never entered into Ethel's little head. But he made no effort to dispel the cloud that had settled over his friend's face.

By and by, Cranbrooke, too, said good night, and went off into his wing, and Max was left alone with his cigar.

The day on the water had verified Max's prediction that it would prove "an opening wedge." Ethel, caught in the tide of the season's gaieties, found herself impelled from one entertainment to the other; their cottage was invaded by callers, their little informal dinners were transformed into banquets of ceremony, as choice and more lively than those of their conventional life in town. The only persons really satisfied by the change of habits in the house were the servants, who, like all artists, require a public to set the seal upon their worth.

Max, bewildered, found himself sometimes accompanying his wife to her parties; oftener—struck with the ghastly inappropriateness of his presence in such haunts—stopping at home and deputing to Cranbrooke the escort of his wife. To his surprise, he perceived that Cranbrooke was not only ready, but eager, on all occasions, to carry Ethel away from him. But then, of course, this was precisely what he had wished.

And Ethel, who lost no opportunity to tell Max how "good," how "lovely," Cranbrooke had been to her, was she not carrying out to the letter her husband's wishes? He observed, moreover, that Ethel was even more impressed than he had expected her to be with that quality of "fascination." Cranbrooke's mind was like a beautiful new country into which she was making excursions, she said once; and Max, after a moment's hesitation, agreed with her very warmly.

At last, Maxwell Pollock awoke one morning, with a start of disagreeable consciousness, to the fact that this was the eve of his thirtieth birthday. Occupied, as he had been with various thoughts that had to do with his transient relations to this sublunary sphere, he had actually allowed himself to lose sight of the swift approach of his day of doom. Now, he arose, took his bath, dressed, and without arousing his wife, who, in the room adjoining, slept profoundly after a gay dance overnight, went alone to the waterside, with the intention of going out in his canoe.

Early as he was, Cranbrooke was before him, carrying the canoe upon his head, moving after the fashion of some queer shell creature down to the float.

Max realized, with a sense of keen self-rebuke, that the spectacle of his friend was repellent to him, and the prospect of a talk alone with Stephen on this occasion, the last thing he would have chosen.

And—evidently a part of the latter-day revolution of affairs—Cranbrooke seemed to have forgotten that this day meant more than another to Pollock. He greeted him cheerily, in commonplace terms, commented on their identity of fancy in the matter of a paddle at sunrise, and offered to relinquish the craft in favor of its owner.

"Of course not. Get in, will you," said Max, throwing off his coat; and, taking one of the paddles, while Cranbrooke plied the other, their swift, even strokes soon carried them far over toward the illuminated east.

When well out upon the bay, they paused to watch the red coming of the sun. Beautiful with matin freshness was the sleeping world around them; and, inspired by the scene, Max, who was kneeling in the bow, turned to exclaim to Cranbrooke, with his old, hearty voice, upon the reward coming to early risers in such surroundings.

"Jove, a man feels born again when he breathes air like this!"

Cranbrooke started. It was almost beyond hope that Max should use such a phrase, in such accents, at such a juncture. Immediately, however, the exhilaration died out of Pollock's manner; and, again turning away his face, he showed that his thoughts had reverted to the old sore spot. He did not see the expression of almost womanly yearning in Cranbrooke's face when the certainty was fixed upon his anxious mind.

The two men talked little, and of casual things only, while aboard. As they returned to the house, Cranbrooke made a movement as if to speak out something burning upon his tongue, and then, repressing it, walked with hasty strides to his own apartment.

The day passed as had done those immediately preceding it. Calls, a party of guests at luncheon, a drive, absorbed Ethel's hours from her husband. When she reached home, at teatime, he had come in from riding, and was standing alone in the hall, awaiting her.

"How nice to find you here alone!" she cried, going up to kiss him, and then taking her place behind the tea tray. "Do sit down, and let us imagine we are back in those dear old days before we were overpowered by outsiders. Never mind! The rush will soon be over; we shall be to ourselves again, you and I and—how stupid I am!" she added, coloring. "You and I, I mean, for he must go back to town."

"You mean Cranbrooke?" he said, as she thought, absent-mindedly, but in reality with something like a cold hand upon his heart, that for a moment gave him a sense of physical apprehension. Had *it* come, he wondered?

But no, this was not physical; this was a shock of purely emotional displeasure. Could he believe his ears, that Ethel, his wife, had indeed blended another than himself with her dream of returning solitude?

"Yes, it will be all over soon," he said, mechanically. "Had you a pleasant drive? And did you enjoy the box seat with Egmont?"

"Oh! Egmont, fortunately, can drive—if he can't *talk*," she answered, lightly. "I suppose I am fastidious, or else spoiled for the conversation of ordinary men, after what I have had recently from Cranbrooke. By the way, Max dear, are you relentless against going with us tonight, to the *fête* at the canoe club? You needn't go inside the clubhouse, you know. It will be lovely to look at, from the water."

"With *us*? Then Cranbrooke has already promised?"

"Yes, of course; he could not leave me in the lurch, could he, when my husband is such an obstinate recluse?"

"And how do you intend to get there?"

"By water, stupid, of course; how else? I will be satisfied with the rowboat, if you won't trust me in a canoe; but Mr. Cranbrooke is such an expert with the paddle, I shouldn't think you would object to letting me go with him. It will be perfectly smooth water, and the air is so mild. Do say I may go in the canoe, dear; it's twice the fun."

"I think you know that, unless I take you, it is my wish that you go nowhere at night in a canoe," he answered, coldly.

Ethel was more hurt at his tone than disappointed by his refusal. She could not think what had come over her husband, of late, so often had this constrained manner presented itself to her advance. She set it down to her unwonted indulgence in society, and promised herself, with a sigh of relinquishment, that, after this summer, she would go back to her life lived for Max alone.

Then, Cranbrooke coming in with two or three visitors, who lingered till almost dinnertime and were persuaded easily to stop for dinner, there was no chance to indulge in meditations, penitential or otherwise. When her guests took their departure, it was in a little steam launch, she and Cranbrooke accompanying the party, and all bound for the *fête*, to be given on a wooded island in the bay. As they were leaving the house, something impelled her to run back and, in the semidarkness of the veranda, seek her husband's side.

"Max darling, kiss me good-bye. Or, if you want me, let me stay with you."

"No, no; I want you to enjoy every moment while you can," he said, withdrawing from her gaze to the shadow of a vine-wreathed column.

"Max, your smile is strange. And once, at dinner, I saw you looking at me, and there was something in your eyes that frightened me. If you hadn't smiled, and lifted your glass to pledge me, I should not have known what to think."

"Ethel! Wife! Do you love me?" he said, catching her to his heart.

"Max! Why, Max! You foolish boy, we shall be seen."

"Tell me, and kiss me once more, my own, my own!"

"They are all aboard except you, Mrs. Pollock," a voice said; and, from the dew of the lawn, Cranbrooke stepped upon the veranda.

Max started violently, and let his wife go from his embrace.

"You know how rude you are making me toward our guests," said Ethel. "You have my wrap, Mr. Cranbrooke? Goodnight, Max; and tomorrow I'll tell you all about it. Better change your mind and come after us, though."

"Max need not trouble to do so," put in Cranbrooke, in a muffled voice. "As usual, I will fill his place."

Max thought he almost hurried her away. They went down the slope of the lawn together; and, at the steep descent leading to the bridge, he saw Ethel stumble, and Cranbrooke throw his arm around her to steady her.

And now, a passion took possession of Maxwell Pollock's being that impelled him to the impetuous action of following them to the wharf, and gesticulating madly after the swift little steamer that bore them away from him.

"He dared take her, did he, when she would have stayed at a word from me? I see all, now. Specious, false, damnably false, he has snared her fancy in his net. But she loves me, I'll swear she loves me, and I'll snatch her from him, if it is with the last effort of my strength. Is there time? Well, what is to come, let it come! While there's life in me, she is mine."

A moment, and he was afloat in the canoe, no sign of weakness in his powerful stroke with the paddle, no thought in his brain but the one intense determination of the male creature to wrest his beloved from the hands of his rival.

Everyone conceded this to be quite the prettiest and most taking event of the season. The rustic clubhouse, its peaked gable and veranda defined with strings of colored lanterns, sent forth the music of the band, while to its portal trooped maidens and cavaliers, landing at the wharf from every variety of craft. The woods behind were linked with chains of light, the shore below lit with bonfires, and more evanescent eruptions of many-hued fireworks. Rockets hissed through the air, and broke in a rain of violet, green, and crimson meteors; till the zenith was a tangled mesh made by the trails of them; fire balloons arose and were lost among the stars; little fire boats, launched from vessels stocked for the purpose, bore their blazing cargoes out upon the tide; other unnamed monsters were let loose to carry apparent destruction zigzagging through the waves. Every attendant yacht, sloop, launch, rowboat, or canoe, with which the water about the island was covered, carried quaint decoration in the guise of Chinese lanterns. Some of the smaller boats were arched with these; others tossed bouquets of fiery bubbles into the air. Creeping about at a snail's pace among the crowded boats, invisible canoes carried silent passengers; an occasional "oh!" of exclamation at the beauty of the scene, the only contribution people felt inclined to make to conversation. It was a pageant of bedazzlement, as if witches, gnomes, spirits of earth, air, and the underworld, had mingled their resources to enchant the eyes of mortals. And over all, sailed the lady moon serenely, forgotten, but sure that her time would come again.

Max found his launch without difficulty, on the outer circle of the amphitheater of light. As he had divined, it was empty, save for two boatmen.

"The ladies went ashore, sir," one of his men said, in answer to his inquiry. "All but Mrs. Pollock, sir."

"Mrs. Pollock? Where is she, then?" he asked, briefly.

"She took our rowboat, sir, and went off on the water with one of the gentlemen. Mr. Cranbrooke, I think it was; and they ordered us to wait just here. No good going ashore, sir, if you want to see. It's better from this point, even, than nearer in."

"Very well," said the master, and at once his canoe moved off to be lost in the crowd.

He had sought for them in vain, peering into all the small boats whenever the flash light of the rockets, or the catharine wheels on the coast, lit the scene. Many a tender interlude was thus revealed; but of the two people he now longed with the fever of madness to discover, he saw nothing.

At last, in a burst from a candle rocket, there was a glimpse of Ethel's red boat cloak, her bare, golden head rising above it. She was sitting in the stern of the rowboat, Cranbrooke beside her, their bow above water, their oars negligently trailing. Ethel's eyes were fixed upon the glittering panorama; but Cranbrooke's eyes were riveted on her.

With an oath, Max drove his paddle fiercely into the sea. The canoe sped forward like an arrow. Blind with anger, he did not observe that he was directly in the track of a little steamer laden with new arrivals, turning in toward the wharf.

A new day dawned before the doctors, who had been all night battling for Maxwell Pollock's life, left him restored to consciousness, and reasonably secure of carrying no lasting ill effect from the blow on his head received by collision with the steamer.

Carried under with his canoe, he had arisen to full view in the glare from a "set piece" of fireworks on the shore, beside the boat containing Cranbrooke and his wife. It was Cranbrooke, not Ethel, who identified the white face coming to the surface within reach of his hand, then sinking again out of sight. It was Cranbrooke, also, who sprang to Pollock's rescue, and, floating with his inert body, was dragged with him aboard the launch.

As the rosy light of the east came to play upon Pollock's features, he opened his eyes for the first time with a look of intelligence. At his bedside, Ethel was kneeling, her whole loving soul in her gaze.

"Is this—I thought it was heaven," he said, feeling for her hand.

"It is heaven for me, now that I have you back, my own darling," she answered, through happy tears.

"A few hours since the accident. The doctors say you will be none the worse for it. And Max dear, only think! This is your birthday! Your thirtieth birthday! Many, many, *many* happy returns!" and she punctuated her wish with warm kisses.

At that juncture, Cranbrooke came into the room and stood at the side of the bed opposite Ethel, who had no eyes for him, but kept on gazing at her recovered treasure as if she could never have enough.

Max, though aware of Stephen's presence, made no movement of recognition, till Ethel spoke in playful chiding.

"Darling! Where are your manners? Aren't you going to speak to our friend, and thank him for saving you—for saving you for *me*, thank God!"

She buried her face in the bedclothes, overcome with the recollection; but even with the exquisite tenderness of her accents thrilling in his ear, Max remained obstinately dumb to Stephen Cranbrooke.

"Forgive him; he is not himself!" pleaded Ethel, as she saw Cranbrooke about to go dejectedly out of the room.

"Someday he will understand me," answered Stephen, with a gallant effort at self-control. Then, withdrawing, he murmured to himself: "But he will never know that, in playing with his edged tools, it is I who have got the death blow."

***Constance C. Harrison** (1843–1920)*

Born in Cumberland, Maryland, and raised in Richmond, Virginia, Constance Cary was a daughter of Old South aristocracy. When she married Burton Harrison, the private secretary of Jefferson Davis, in 1867, the two moved to New York City with other "Confederate carpetbaggers," in search of new identities and financial opportunities after the defeat of the South. While her husband established a successful law practice, Mrs. Harrison became a prolific writer. In scores of articles and over thirty books of essays, short stories, plays, and novels, she waxed romantic about southern society and satirical about northern manners. Bar Harbor was a favorite summer resort for the family, and it became a locale for her stories after the Harrisons built their cottage, Sea Urchins, in the 1880s.

About the Muethers

John and Kathryn Muether's fondness for the literature of Mount Desert developed from their frequent visits to Bar Harbor. When they are not vacationing in coastal Maine, they live in central Florida. John serves as library director and professor of church history at Reformed Theological Seminary in Oviedo, and Kathryn is the librarian of the Geneva School in Winter Park. They have four children, and this is their first literary collaboration.